Terror in the Trees
By
Chris Olsen

THURSDAY

1

"MOM, where are my hiking shoes?" yelled Steve.

"I don't know, have you looked in the garage?"

Steve went out to the garage and saw his shoes sitting next to the four wheeler, and hoped they would fit. Last weekend his parents had asked him to try his hiking boots on, but he was too busy playing Call of Duty with his friends and never actually tried them on. He sat down on the four wheeler and slid his foot into his hiking boot, they fit!

Steve Jacobs and his family were getting ready to go on their first camping trip of the summer break. It was a family tradition to go the weekend after Memorial Day because there were less people out. His sister Clara wasn't as excited to go. She was a teenager who would rather sit and talk with her friends than hang out with her family. George, Steve's father, was a professor teaching Physics at Idaho State College and his mother was a second grade teacher at Middleton Elementary. The school year had been very busy and they were all looking forward to a more relaxing summer.

After trying on his boots Steve went out to see if his dad George needed any help hooking the truck up to the trailer.

"Dad, do you need any help getting the truck hooked up?"

"No I'm just finishing up, why don't you go get the four wheeler out of the garage and pull it up to the back of the trailer and we will get it loaded."

Steve ran back to the garage and started the four wheeler. He was excited because this was the first time he had been asked to load the four wheeler by himself.

Just as he started pulling the four wheeler out of the garage his older sister Clara came out the door, "Steve what are you doing? You aren't supposed to be driving the four wheeler".

"Mind your own business Clara, Dad told me to drive it over to the back of the trailer so we can load it up," Steve said.

Clara rolled her eyes and headed to the trailer with her bag of clothes.

As Steve pulled the four wheeler out of the driveway and lined it up with the ramp on the back of the trailer his dad came over to help him.

"Alright pal, do you think you can pull the four wheeler up the ramp and into the trailer without damaging anything?"

"Yeah I can do it."

"Alright give me a minute to get the mat rolled out so you can park on it."

George walked up the ramp and rolled out the black mat that they would place on the floor so they could keep the floor clean.

"Alright son go ahead and slowly come up the ramp, watch where you're going and listen to me, I will tell you when to stop."

Steve slowly began pulling the four wheeler up the ramp making sure that he wasn't going to hit the folded up benches on either side.

"That is perfect go ahead and turn the four wheeler off and set the parking brake" his dad yelled.

Steve turned off the four wheeler and they finished securing the four wheeler and closed the back ramp.

George and Steve headed back into the house to see if Maggie needed any help loading up the rest of the groceries for the camping trip. "Hey honey everything is loaded up except whatever you still have in here. What can we help you with?"

"I have everything packed into these grocery sacks if you can just help me get them into the trailer" Maggie replied.

"Sure thing honey, I will have Steve grab the ice out of the freezer and load it and the drinks into the cooler while you & I carry these out"

Steve walked out to the garage as Clara was coming into the house. " Hey Clara, will you help me load the ice and drinks into the cooler?"

"Ugh you're so helpless you little dweeb" Clara replied.

She then walked over and they grabbed the ice and drinks and headed to the trailer. As they were loading the cooler Clara's phone chimed. She put the drinks down and grabbed her phone. "Hey can't you check that after we are done?" Steve asked.

"Shut Up dweeb this is an important text from Rachel, I need to text her back."

Just then George and Maggie walked into the trailer with the remaining groceries.

"Clara, how are you going to survive without phone service?" George asked. Clara just rolled her eyes at him.

"Her heart will probably stop the second we enter the canyon," Steve said with a chuckle.

Clara shoved Steve and he fell into the cooler.

"Knock it off you three, we are going to have a fun camping trip, whether you like it or not," Maggie said.

"Oh we are just giving her a hard time," George replied. "Alright everyone grab their things that they need in the truck and get in.

Steve ran in the house and grabbed his Ipad while Maggie and Clara climbed in the truck. Steve came back out of the house and was running over to the truck when Sadie, the neighbor's dog ran over to greet him and almost knocked him over. "Geez Sadie you almost knocked me over." Steve said as he patted Sadie on the head and Clara laughed at him. "Come on Sadie, I will take you home." Steve grabbed her collar and led her back over to the neighbors back yard and locked the gate.

George climbed in the truck and closed the garage. "Alright, is everyone ready to go?" he asked.

They all replied with a resounding "YES!"

As they started down the road Maggie asked Steve "did you remember your bag?"

"Crap!!!"

George rolled his eyes and went around the block stopping in front of the house. "Go grab your bag you idiot" said Clara.

"Don't talk to your brother that way!" replied Maggie.

Steve jumped out of the door and ran into the house to grab his bag.

A few minutes later Steve was back in the truck and George asked once again "Alright, NOW is everyone ready to go?"

They all replied with a resounding "YES!" And they headed down the road.

2

After driving through nothing but fields and small towns for two and a half hours the family finally entered the last town they would be seeing before entering the canyon. Cherryton was a small Rocky Mountain college town that seemed to alway be busy especially during the Universities semesters. George slowly pulled over into a gas station to fill up the truck before heading up the canyon.

"Alright you two run into the gas station with your mom and grab us some snacks and drinks for the ride up the canyon, we still have about an hour to go before we get to the camp spot."

Maggie, Clara, & Steve all got out of the truck and headed into the gas station.

"Alright grab a drink and ONE snack for the ride, I will get something for myself and your dad."

Steve already knew what he was going to get, his favorite candy bar was a Kit Kat and for a drink he wanted a Dr. Pepper. Clara wanted an Arizona Iced Tea and a Hershey Bar. Maggie grabbed herself and George each a Coke & Snickers bar.

"Does everyone have what they need?" Maggie asked.

Both kids shook their heads yes and put their items on the counter. While the cashier was ringing the items up and Maggie was paying Steve noticed a headline in the Cherryton Journal stating **"College students claim they were chased by a giant animal in Chapel Fork up Cherryton Canyon, campers warned to watch for anything unusual."**

"Mom, look at this."

Maggie looked down as the cashier handed her the change and responded "Oh it is probably just some headline trying to get you to buy the journal, it's nothing to worry about."

She handed Steve a quarter and said "Now come on, your dad is waiting."

"Hey mom look, this is one of the new quarters with the National Parks on it. This one has Yellowstone on it. Cool!"

"That's neat, you will have to save that one."

"Do you think we could clean this pink paint off of it when we get home?"

"Yes, I'm sure your dad can get it cleaned up and polished."

George had been a coin collector when he was younger and had all the necessary tools to make a coin look new.

They all headed back to the truck where George was waiting.

"Dad you should have seen the headline in the newspaper, it said that a few college kids were chased by a giant animal up Cherryton Canyon."

"Oh really, that is interesting!"

"What's Steve talking about?" George whispered to Maggie.

"I'm sure it's nothing but a few overzealous youngsters drinking too much on a camping trip" she replied.

"Alright kids let's get going I'm sure your Aunt, Uncle & cousins are getting set up and waiting for us to arrive. If we don't hurry Grandma & Grandpa will beat us to the campsite as well" George said.

Charles & Gloria Jacobs were notorious for being late and George always gave them a hard time so the last thing he wanted to do was get to camp after them.

They all buckled in and George turned back onto the highway to head up the canyon. He always loved this drive. First they would pass Cherryton University and then they would head into the canyon with steep ledges, aspen, and pine trees lining the road.

As they passed the University into the mouth of the canyon they noticed the police had a green Subaru Outback stopped with what looked to be students from the University. The students were being very animated with what they were describing to the officers. "I wonder what that is about," Clara asked.

"They are probably just trying to get out of a ticket," George said.

"Maybe they saw the beast that is living up the canyon," Steve replied.

"Oh Steve there is nothing scary up the canyon other than your uncle without his shirt on." Maggie said as they all laughed.

The canyon was beautiful! All of the Aspen trees were just beginning to get their leaves and they looked like a patchwork mixed into the pines. Most of the wildflowers were just starting to bloom and the river was raging after a heavy snow packed winter. It was a winter that these mountains hadn't seen in roughly ten years.

"Look guys there is a moose" Clara said. It was the first time that she had taken her ear buds out and put her phone down for the entire ride. The moose was standing about 100 ft above them on a cliff eating aspen shoots.

"WOW, I haven't seen a moose that close to the highway in years. I bet with all of the snow the animals up here had a rough winter and headed toward the lower end of the canyon where there was less snow" George said.

"That or they are running from the beast that lives up in the canyon."

"Steve enough with that story, there is nothing up this canyon. I don't want you to mention anything to your cousins about that stupid headline, do you understand me?"

"Yes mom, but do you think the beast looks like bigfoot or the beast from *Beauty & the Beast*?" Steve replied.

"I'm serious, you will scare the daylights out of them and they won't leave their trailer. Do you understand me?"

"Yes mom."

As they continued up the winding road Steve was watching out the window for anything strange up on the mountain sides. He didn't see much other than trees and a mule deer grazing on the wildflower leaves.

" I wonder if there are bears up here? Maybe it was a bear that chased those students?" He thought to himself.

3

Rob, a senior at Cherryton University, his girlfriend Becky, a junior, and his best friend Jake, also a senior, had chased after a police car for roughly 10 miles before they finally got his attention and stopped him at the mouth of Cherryton canyon. They all jumped out screaming as a truck and trailer went by headed up the canyon.

Officer Terry Johnson got out of his car but was unable to understand a thing the three were saying. "It's too early for this shit he thought." It was only Thursday and after Memorial Day weekend he was hoping this weekend would be uneventful.

"ALRIGHT EVERYONE CALM DOWN" he yelled. "I need you to speak one at a time and tell me why you are so frantic.

As he looked the three over he noticed one of them had a scrape on his face and a black eye.

"We were camping up near Aspen Grove last night and something tried to drag me out of camp," Jake said.

"Were you in a tent or where were you sleeping?"

"No, I had passed out by the campfire sometime during the night and I woke up and a large beast was trying to pull me out of the camp by my foot. I tried to kick it and it swatted me with its hand and the next thing I remember is Rob waking me up near the tree line of the campsite."

Officer Johnson had a skeptical look on his face.

"He is being serious, I found him early this morning laying out in the weeds and he had blood coming down his face. Are you sure you didn't run into a tree branch last night and fall down? I mean if you were drunk enough to pass out by the fire maybe you got up looking for your tent and while walking through the trees you hit a branch."

"No, I remember being dragged by some sort of creature through the camp."

"My best guess is that you had too much to drink and had a nightmare. There are two species of animals that are big enough to drag someone your size out of a camp, a mountain lion or a black bear. If either of those animals had smacked you like you said their claws would have ripped your face open at the very least."

"Look Officer we aren't lying when I woke up this morning and got out of the tent both Rob and Jake looked terrified. Something tried to drag Jake out of camp" Becky interjected.

"Alright this is the second report we have had like this so I would like you all to come down to the station and file a report. This way we can document both cases and see what we find in common."

"Wait this already happened to someone and you haven't found anything?" Becky said.

"Two days ago we received a call from some kids that had been up the canyon smoking weed and they swore up and down that they were chased by a large animal. But that happened in Chapel Fork which is at least 5 miles from where you were camping. Follow me down to the station so we can get your statements and then you can head home."

They all got back in the car and followed Officer Johnson back to the police station.

4

It was just before noon as George slowed down as he saw the sign for Fredericks Basin, the canyon that the family was camping in. He waited for oncoming traffic to pass and then made a left hand turn onto the dirt road; they had about six miles left to go before they reached the campground. The bumpy road was just damp enough to keep the dust down as they drove toward the campground. Since the road was only one lane with pull offs every once in a while George was hoping there wouldn't be much traffic.

Groves of aspen trees lined both sides of the road with Cherryton river running along the right hand side of the road. The river was running fast & high. As the Jacobs family drove down the first few miles of road they saw a couple of beaver ponds and even happened to see a beaver swimming in one of them.

"Clara put your phone away and look at the beautiful wilderness around you."

Clara rolled her eyes "I know mom we have been here before, I have seen it."

"The canyon changes every year and the wildlife definitely doesn't stay in one spot, it would do you good to get away from the screen Clara," Maggie replied.

Clara sighed and put her phone down.

" I don't know why they care so much if I play games on my phone, it's not like I'm affecting them" she thought to herself.

She would have liked to have been at home hanging out with her friends and watching Tik Tok videos but instead she had to go camping with her family and now wouldn't have cell service until they left in four days. While sitting and watching the trees go by she thought of the past camping trips and realized that they usually had fun on the trips and may as well make the best of it.

"Steve, did you bring your laser tag guns?" she asked.

"Dang it, I knew I forgot something."

"I put new batteries in them last weekend and put them in the trailer."

"Thanks Dad!"

We should ask Joey and Marie if they want to place laser tag tonight, it was a lot of fun last year."

"Wow is that enthusiasm from Clara" Maggie said with a chuckle.

"Look at the elk up on the face of the mountain" George said as he slowed the truck. A few hundred yards up the hill side a group of 30 or so elk walked out of a grove of pine trees.

"Steve, grab my binoculars from under your seat and hand them to me."

He grabbed the binoculars and handed them to his dad. As George looked over the herd he noticed there was a bull in velvet.

"There is a nice bull elk up there. He is at the back of the herd just coming out of the trees."

He handed the binoculars to Maggie "they are such beautiful animals, here Clara take a look."

Clara looked at the elk for a minute or so and handed the binoculars to Steve. "Dad, why do his antlers look like they have fur on them?" Steve asked.

"It's because they are in what is called velvet. The antlers fall off every winter and the elk regrow the antlers in the spring and early summer. When they are growing they have a skin over them called velvet. Once they are done growing and hardening they scrape the velvet off their antlers."

"Wow, that is cool!" Steve said.

George started slowly driving the truck down the road again as the rest of the family looked out the windows to see if they could spot any more wildlife.

About half a mile from where George's brother Mike told them they were going to stay they passed a camp that looked like it had been trashed, the coolers and chairs were tipped over and a fold up plastic picnic table looked like a Cow had decided to sit down on it, the legs were crushed into the ground and that bench had been bent.

"Dad, look over there WHAT HAPPENED?" Steve asked.

"I don't know son you guys stay in the truck and I'm going to go check it out" George said as he stopped the truck.

"Honey I don't know if that is a good idea."

"Everything will be fine I'm sure it is nothing, but you guys stay in the truck just in case."

George slowly headed over to the campsite while looking around in the trees, he didn't see anything out of the norm so he went over to the trailer and knocked on the door. Nobody answered so he knocked again, still nothing. He walked around to the other side of the trailer and down into the trees toward the river, he knew quite a few moose called this area home and they could be temperamental so he moved slowly through the trees.. Suddenly there was a thrashing in the brush coming towards him. He moved over behind the tree expecting something large to be charging him. A few seconds later a Heifer and its calf walked out of the trees towards the river. George sighed "Damn cows!"

This area was a free range area and there were a lot of cows brought up here by ranchers for the summer.

He headed back to the truck and Maggie asked "Did you see anything?"

"No, a few cows that made me about shit myself but that was it."

"Dad, what do you think knocked everything over?" Clara asked.

"It was probably the monster that was chasing people," Steve said in an excited voice.

"STEVE enough with the monster story" Maggie said.

"It was probably those cows wandering through the camp that knocked everything over, they have been known to do that. These campers probably left their trailer over from last weekend to save them a spot, so it serves them right," George said as he put the truck in drive and headed down the road.

5

As they rounded the final bend they saw Mike & Katrina's trailer. Joey & Marie came running up the road excited to see their cousins, Joey was twelve just like Steve and Marie was ten. George slowed the truck down and rolled down his window "Hey you rugrats it's good to see you! Will you go stand by your trailer so I don't have to worry about running you over?"

"Can Clara and Steve get out of the truck, Uncle George?" Joey asked.

"Let me get backed in and then we will all get out. Does that sound ok?"

"Yep! Come on Marie, let's get out of the way."

George started backing the trailer in and Mike came over and helped guide him into the correct spot. They all got out of the truck and went to greet Mike, Katrina, Joey, & Marie. Mike went over to the cooler and grabbed himself and George a beer. "Good to see you brother" Mike said as he handed George the beer.

"It's good to see you too, I see you got set up ok. When is Mom & Dad supposed to be here?"

"They said they would be here around 1pm so in another hour or so."

They walked to the back of the truck and started unhooking the trailer while Steve, Marie, & Joey went running down to the river to see if they could spot any fish. Maggie, Clara, & Katrina went and sat down in the shade. "How are you Clara? You have grown at least 2 inches since last time I saw you."

Clara smiled and said "I'm doing good Aunt Katrina, just glad to be done with school."

"I can't believe you're going to be a sophomore next year! Your parents are getting old." Katrina gave Maggie a wink and smiled.

All of a sudden they heard a scream from down by the river. Mike and George took off down to the river and Maggie, Katrina, & Clara were not far behind. As they all came down the hill to the river, Marie was crawling out of the river soaking wet.

"Mom, Joey pushed me into the river" she said with a whimper.

"I didn't mean to, she was reaching down to grab a stick out of the water and I was trying to scare her."

"Joey you know better than that, now your sister is cold and wet," Mike said.

"I'm sorry Marie, it was an accident."

"It's ok" she said while her lips quivered from being cold as Katrina took her back to the trailer to get changed.

"Alright boys why don't you go look for firewood" George said.

"Be careful and don't go too far from camp," Maggie said.

Steve & Joey headed down a trail towards a group of trees looking for any branches that had broken off during the winter or any trees that had fallen down that their dads could cut up with a chainsaw.

As they entered a group of pine trees they felt the coolness of the shade and the softness of the ground covered in pine needles below their feet. Every once in a while they could hear the chipmunks chirping up in the trees.

"Hey Joey, do you want to hear something cool?"

"Yeah what is it?"

"If I tell you you can't tell anyone, especially Marie. My mom told me if I scared you guys I would be grounded for life."

"What is it? I promise I won't tell her."

"Ok, so we stopped by the gas station in Cherryton this morning to fill up on gas and get a snack. When we went into the store there was a headline about some kids getting chased by some sort of creature up Cherryton Canyon. My mom said it was probably just a headline to try and get you to buy the newspaper, but what if it is something else?"

"What do you think it could be?"

"I don't know, maybe a bear or maybe some sort of monster?"

"Oh give me a break Steve, we all know there are no such things as monsters and there aren't very many bears around here. I don't think our parents have ever even seen one."

All of a sudden they heard rustling in the brush just outside of the pine trees and something black move back into the brush.

"What do you think it is Steve?"

"I don't know, probably a dumb cow or something. Come on, let's go look."

"I don't think that is a good idea. We should head back to camp."

"I thought you didn't believe in monsters or bears being around here?"

"Well I don't but you never know maybe it is a moose or something that is going to stomp on us."

"Yeah you're right that would be bad, let's go back to camp, but remember not a word about the story or my mom will ring my neck!"

6

"George, will you please get the 4-wheeler unloaded so we can finish setting the trailer up?" Maggie asked.

"Yes sweetie I will go do it right after Mike & I finish our drinks."

"So Mike, how has work been? I'm guessing the building market is getting busy this time of year, especially for a great contractor like you."

"Yeah it has been pretty busy, we are currently in the process of building three houses with another five scheduled for the summer."

"WOW you aren't going to get much time for camping are you?"

"Ah we will sneak away a few times. There is alway room for fun."

"How is the University life now that you are officially a professor?"

"It's going well, I'm not teaching any summer classes so that is nice."

"Are you just teaching Physics classes or other subjects as well?"

"I taught two Intro to Physics classes this last semester, but I will be taking on more of a load this fall since we have a professor that is retiring. Alright I suppose I better go get the four wheeler unloaded so Maggie can finish unpacking the trailer, do you mind helping me since the boys are off in the woods?"

They both got up and went and opened the back door of the trailer to roll out the four wheeler. "Alright I'm going to go up into the trailer and unhook it if you will help guide me down?" "Sounds good to me, I will just stand here and give directions," Mike said with a laugh.

Katrina came out of her and Mike's trailer after getting Marie changed. She carried two glasses of lemonade over to where Maggie was sitting under some aspen trees.

"Isn't this place beautiful this time of year" Katrina said as she handed Maggie a glass of lemonade.

"Thank you for the lemonade, yes it is beautiful. I could sit and listen to the Aspen leaves rustle all day long!"

"So Maggie, are you glad to be done teaching for the summer?"

"Yes and no, I had a good 2nd grade class this year so I will miss the students but I'm glad to have some time off and enjoy the summer with the kids. In only a few years Clara will be off to college."

"I can't believe that, it seems like yesterday you were putting her in her playpen for a nap during our camping trips."

"I know time sure flies. The days sometimes go by slowly, but you blink and the year is over."

"How is your job at the hospital? Is it as busy now as it was this winter?"

"It is going well, patient numbers have come down to a normal level. Which is nice after all of the sickness we saw this winter."

"Mom, do you know where the boys went?" Clara asked.

"They went off that way to see if they could find any wood for the fire tonight. I'm sure knowing them they are off running around trying to find ways to get hurt."

"Is it ok if I go look for them? I'm getting bored just sitting around camp."

"I don't want you to go off on your own, why don't you stay here. Your grandparents will be here soon and they will need our help unloading."

"Mom, I'm almost fifteen I will be fine."

"Just make sure you are back in thirty minutes whether you find them or not. You guys haven't had lunch yet and it's almost 2. We should probably eat something since we won't be having dinner for a while."

Clara headed off down the trail that the boys had taken hoping they hadn't gone too far. As much as she hated to admit it she was kind of nervous after reading the headline in the newspaper.

7

It was just after 1p.m. when Rob, Becky, Jake finished giving their statements to Officer Johnson and they were exhausted. After writing down their accounts of what happened Terry told them they were free to go and that he would be in contact.

As they were walking back to the car Jake asked if they could go back up the canyon to look for his phone.

"Are you kidding me? There is no way I'm going back up there today after what happened last night."

"Look Becky, that phone is only two months old and my dad is going to kill me if I tell him not only was I attacked by some creature while passed out in the woods, but I also lost the phone he just bought me."

Jake came from a hard working ranching family that lived in Princeton Idaho which was located in the same valley just up the road from Cherryton. While they weren't poor they were taught to value their items and always be aware of your surroundings especially when in the woods.

"Jake, let's take Becky home and then we will stop by our apartment and grab my gun and head up the canyon."

"Babe I don't want you going back up there after what happened."

"We will be fine, it won't get dark until about 7 and we should be home by then," Rob stated as they all climbed in the car. A few minutes later they were pulling up to Becky's apartment.

"Be careful out there please," Becky said as she leaned over and gave Rob a kiss.

"We will be, don't worry I will be back over here by eight or nine."

Becky climbed out of the car and headed to her apartment on the second floor. She opened the door, threw her bag down and collapsed on the couch. She laid there thinking about the last twenty four hours and everything that had happened and couldn't believe that Rob and Jake were headed back up the canyon. Soon she began drifting to sleep but she kept thinking about what it could have been that dragged Jake out of the camp. Officer Johnson was correct the only thing it could have been was a bear or a mountain lion and both would have ripped his face open with its claws.

Becky got up and went to the kitchen. She poured herself a glass of lemonade and grabbed a few crackers and a couple of slices of cheese. While she enjoyed her snack she looked out the window in a daze at the kids playing in the playground. After she finished her snack she walked over to the couch and laid down. She turned on the tv and let the background noise from one of the talk shows that were on lull her to sleep.

Rob and Jake pulled up to their apartment, grabbed the camping stuff they had brought home and headed inside.

"I'm going to take a quick shower to get this dirt and dried blood off of me," Jake said.

"Ok, sounds good, I'm going to go put some of my stuff away and grab my gun."

Rob then headed into his bedroom and unpacked his bag. He reached under his bed and pulled out his lockbox where he kept his pistol. He put the box on his bed, opened it up and grabbed his pistol and ammunition. After grabbing his gun, a 40 caliber Smith and Wesson, a jacket ,and a hat he headed into the kitchen to get a drink.

He opened up the fridge, grabbed a cold beer and sat down at the table. He cracked open the can and took a big swig. He was hoping it would help his nerves calm down a bit. Even though he was acting like he wasn't nervous to head back up the canyon he was. When he saw Jake sprawled out on the ground this morning with blood on his face he thought he was dead. He thought to himself "How didn't I hear the commotion last night? I shouldn't have drank so much, dad always told me to be aware of my surroundings especially out in the wilderness."

Jake came out of the bathroom with a towel wrapped around him and looked over at Rob.

"Hey man, do you mind grabbing me one of those while I go and get changed?"

"Yeah no problem, but we better get going soon so we can get up the canyon and back down before it gets dark. I don't want to be up there after that."

"Absolutely, I will drink it quickly and then we can head back up." Jake headed to his bedroom and started getting dressed. Rob got up and headed to the fridge to grab Jake's beer. Just as he closed the fridge his phone began to ring so he sat the beer on the counter and jogged into the living room expecting to see Becky's number on his caller id. When he realized it wasn't her number he let it ring a couple more times deciding whether to answer it or not. He finally picked it up and swiped across the screen to answer it.

"Hello."

"Rob?"

"This is him."

"Rob, this is Officer Johnson, are you with Jake?"

"Yes I am, is something wrong?"

"No, nothing is wrong. I just had a few follow up questions for him and he isn't answering his phone."

"Oh yeah, his phone got lost up the canyon, I'm guessing that when he was being dragged across the ground it fell out of his pocket."

"Ok, can I talk to him?"

"He just got out of the shower and is getting dressed, can I have him call you back?"

"Yes, that would be great, thanks!"

"No problem, talk to you later." Rob hung up the phone just as Jake came out of his bedroom. "Hey man, that was Officer Johnson. He has a few questions for you and needs you to call him back."

Jake sighed, "Alright I will call him back as soon as I finish this beer."

They both sat down at the kitchen table feeling exhausted.

Rob broke the silence after a few minutes, "What do you think is up there, this is so crazy. I thought you were dead when I came out of the tent this morning."

"I don't know what it was. It was big and black so it couldn't have been a black bear, but then again I was drunk so my vision may have been blurry. Look Rob if you don't want to go back up there with me that is fine, but I need to go find my phone or my dad is going to kill me."

"There is no way I'm going to let you go back up there alone, why don't you go call Officer Johnson and then we will head up. We are going to need to hurry because it's already almost three."

Rob handed Jake his phone and Jake dialed the number on Officer Johnson's card. Rob decided he needed some fresh air so he headed outside so Jake could have some space while talking to Officer Johnson.

8

Steve and Joey left the grove of pine trees and headed back to camp. They were walking down the trail checking behind them every once in a while to make sure whatever had been in the shrubs wasn't following them. The last thing they wanted was to be trampled by a moose.

"Ssshhh. I think I hear something coming down the trail," Steve said as he knelt down.

"Are you just trying to scare me? I didn't hear anything."

"No I heard something walking down the trail, come on lets hide in the brush." They both crawled into the brush that was next to the trail. They were hoping if it was a cow or some other animal it would just walk right by them. Steve was trying to see what was coming but couldn't see more than fifty feet down the trail.

"Hey look Joey" Steve whispered.

"It's Clara, let's scare her when she walks by, stay quiet."

Clara was wandering down the trail, she could see the pine grove from where she was but didn't see the boys.

"Steve, Joey where are you?" She yelled, but didn't get an answer.

When Clara called for them she was no further than ten feet away from the boys but they didn't move and Joey had to resist the urge to giggle. Steve thought for sure she had seen them when she yelled their names. She continued walking past them headed for the pine trees.

Once Clara had passed them. Steve jumped up and went running at Clara.

"BOOOOO."

Clara jumped about tripping over a tree root that crossed the trail.

"GOD DAMN IT STEVE."

Both the boys fell on the ground cackling away. Clara went up to Steve and smacked him on the head. "OW he said, I'm telling Mom you swore and hit me."

"You scared the crap out of me you idiot."

"Were you afraid that it was the big monster from the newspaper?" Steve said with a giggle.

Clara looked over at Joey and he was smirking.

"Steve, did you tell Joey about that? Mom told you not to tell Joey or Marie."

"No, I didn't tell him anything."

"You're a liar, I saw Joey smirking."

"Fine I told him, but he isn't going to tell anyone about it."

Clara reached over and smacked him again.

"That's it I'm going to go tell Mom you hit me twice and swore."

"Perfect, let's go back together and I will tell her how you told Joey about the newspaper headline and you will be grounded for a month."

Steve sighed, "Fine I won't tell her you hit me if you don't tell her I told Joey. Joey promised to keep it a secret, didn't you Joey?"

Joey nodded his head yes.

"Alright you guys let's go explore this place. We need to hurry because Mom said we need to be back to the trailer for lunch by 2:30."

"Clara, I don't think we want to head that way, we saw something in the bushes," Joey said.

"What are you afraid it's Bigfoot?" Clara said in a sarcastic voice.

"No but what if it is a moose and it tries to trample us?" Joey said.

"A moose? Sweet, let's go see if we can get a picture of it," Clara said as she pulled out her phone and headed down the trail with the boys in tow.

As they walked into the grove of pines Clara asked "alright you two where did you see this big monster?"

"It was over there in that thick willow brush on the outside of the trees" Steve said.

Clara headed over towards the willows and started walking through them. She got a few feet in when they all heard a big crash and jumped back. Pretty soon they saw a flash of black about fifty yards away running through the brush towards the river.

"Dang it, I was hoping to get a picture of it, it has to be a moose!"

"Alright Clara I've had enough fun lets head back to the trailer I'm really getting hungry" Steve said.

"Fine let's go, Mom will be wondering where we are anyways."

9

Clara, Steve, & Joey wandered back to camp looking up at the hillside trying to see if they could see the moose, but there was no sign. As they walked into camp Maggie looked over and saw them coming down the trail.

"Hey kiddos you guys ready for lunch?"

"Yeah I'm starving," Steve said.

"Ok I will go make you a plate with chips and sandwiches. Joey, do you want one as well?'

"Yes please."

"Ok go ask Marie if she wants one. I think she is still in your trailer."

Joey wandered over to their trailer and peaked his head inside. Marie was sitting at the table playing a game on her tablet.

"Hey dork, do you want aunt Maggie to make you a sandwich?"

"Don't call me a dork you scumbag, I'm sitting here trying to get warm since you tried to drown me in the river!"

Joey rolled his eyes. "Do you want a sandwich or not?"

"Yes I do but tell aunt Maggie no mustard."

Joey ran out of the trailer and over to aunt Maggie's.

"Aunt Maggie, Marie said she wants a sandwich with EXTRA mustard."

"Oh Joey, you are just like Steve, always picking on your sister. I know she doesn't like mustard. Now go help Steve set up the folding picnic table and I will bring these out to you."

Joey smirked and went to the back of the trailer with Steve and they grabbed the picnic table.

"Be careful not to pinch your fingers," Maggie yelled.

"We will be mom," Steve said.

George and Mike were still sitting over by Mike's trailer talking.

"When do you think Mom & Dad will get here?" George asked.

"Oh you know how they are, they are never on time anywhere. They said they would be here earlier but I never expected them to get to camp until at least three".

"Yeah you're right they are always running late." George said with a laugh.

"Looks like the boys are already having a blast," Mike said.

"Yes it does, it reminds me of when we were kids up here running around and trying to find secret hideaways."

" So Mike, did you see the headline in the newspaper this morning?"

"No I didn't, we left early and didn't stop anywhere on the way up. What was it about?"

"Ah it's probably nothing, but I wanted you to know in case Steve opens his big mouth and scares your kids." George then proceeded to tell Mike about the headline.

Mike laughed. "I'm sure it was some college kids up here having a good time and taking some shrooms or some other drugs."

"Yeah that is probably exactly what happened," George said while laughing.

"Anyways I just wanted to let you know in case your kids wake up scared in the middle of the night."

"Oh it's no big deal do you remember the scary stories we used to tell with our cousins while we were camping? Man, I remember some nights not being able to sleep at all," Mike said.

10

As the phone rang all Jake could think about was whether the Sheriff's Dept. was calling to tell him they had figured out what tried to drag him away or if they were going to call him in for questioning again.

"Hello Officer Johnson speaking."

" Hi Officer this is Jake, Rob said you wanted to speak to me."

"Yes, I just wanted to go over last night's events one more time so I can make sure I have the story straight before handing the reports over to the Department of Fish and Game."

"Wait, you guys aren't even going to look into what happened?"

"Since we believe this is an incident involving an animal we need to have the Department of Fish and Game take the lead on the case and if they need our help they will get us involved. I promise you Officer Campbell will do a great job with the investigation and keep you informed."

"Ok." Jake said with a sigh. "What do you need to know?"

"I would like you to begin from the beginning last night when you first arrived and what events happened from then until this morning when I talked to you."

"Yesterday around two in the afternoon Rob called me to see if I wanted to go camping for the night once he got off work. I said sure and let him know I would get things packed up so when he got home we would be able to head up the canyon. Rob arrived home around four and we loaded our camping stuff into the car and picked up Becky.

After we picked up Becky we stopped at the grocery store and bought some food and beer. We headed up the canyon and arrived at our camp spot around 6:45. We then set up our tent and played horseshoes before starting dinner."

"What did you have for dinner?"

"We ate hamburgers and hotdogs with potato chips."

"Ok good to know thank you, please proceed with the remainder of the night."

"Once we were done eating it was getting chilly so we started our campfire and sat around playing poker on a small table that we had brought. Around nine I went to the car, turned on some music and got out a bottle of whisky that I had brought up to the camp. We all took a swig and continued to listen to music and play cards until probably about 10:30. After that we sat around the fire and talked for a little bit. I was cold so I grabbed a blanket and laid on the ground next to the fire. The next thing I remember is being woken up as I was dragged away from the camp by whatever it was that had grabbed a hold of me. It was dark and the moon was no longer up so I didn't get a good view of what it was. I remember trying to kick it away as it continued to drag me towards the trees. It then took a swipe at my face and that is the last thing I remembered before Rob woke me up this morning.

When I woke up Rob was kneeling over me and had a panicked look on his face and was asking what had happened. He then helped me to a chair by the fire and Becky brought me some water. He again asked me what had happened and slowly it was coming back so I told him the story. Both Becky and Rob were just as terrified as I was and we wanted to get out of there so we packed up all of our stuff and got in the car and headed down the canyon. Not too far after we got on the main road we saw you and tried to chase you down until you finally pulled over."

"Ok thanks. I just have a few follow up questions for you. After cooking dinner last night did you guys put the grill away or had you left it out?"

"We had left it out, I know we should have put it away so animals didn't come around but bears haven't been seen around there very often and we didn't think much of it."

"It's fine I just need all the details so we can do our best to investigate. Next, how much did you have to drink throughout the night? Were you totally plastered or a little buzzed?"

"I would say I was in the middle. I think I had three beers and two shots but that was over the entire night so I definitely was buzzed but I wasn't blackout drunk."

"Ok thanks for all the information. I will send the reports over to Officer Campbell right now and he should reach out to you in the next day or two."

Jake hung up the phone and thought to himself "Should I have told him we were going back up there to look for my phone?"

He decided it didn't matter and besides, even if Officer Johnson had told him not to go back up there he would have gone anyway, he would never hear the end of it if he didn't bring his phone back home.

He then headed outside to find Rob who was sitting outside in a lawn chair waiting for him.

"That took a while. Are we in trouble for supposedly lying to them."

"No we are not in trouble, Officer Johnson has to turn the case over to the Fish & Game and wants to make sure he has everything covered in his report."

"What did he say about us going back up the canyon?"

"I didn't tell him, I figured it didn't matter as it wasn't part of the details from last night"

"Probably a good idea he may have told us not to go back up."

They both headed back into the apartment and drank the last of their beers before grabbing their jackets and Rob's gun. It was just after four when they got into Rob's car to head back up the canyon. As they climbed in the car Rob grabbed his phone and sent a quick text to Becky telling her that Officer Johnson had called again so they were getting a late start.

11

It was just after five and Charles and Gloria were sitting on the side of the road next to the Aspen Grove turnoff. They were already running late and just blew a tire on the way to meet their family for a camping trip up in Fredericks Basin. They were supposed to be up there around 1 but as usual they never left on time. Charles was out on the side of the road getting his jack out of the back of his truck when a car pulled up behind him and two young men got out of the car.

"Hi sir, do you need some help?"

"That would be great. I'm already running late. I was supposed to meet my son's and their families 3 hours ago. Thank you so much for the help! What are your names?"

"I'm Rob and this is my friend Jake. We are on our way to go find his phone up Aspen Grove, he left it there last night."

"Oh I see you had a wild night last night huh?" Charles said with a laugh.

"It's a long story but yes something like that." Jake said while looking at Rob.

He was having a hard time deciding whether to tell anyone about their story or not since it seemed so crazy.

"I've had a few of those myself in my younger days."

Rob grabbed the jack from Charles' truck and went to the back of the trailer, one of the rear wheels was flat. He jacked the trailer up while Charles and Jake watched. Once he jacked the truck up he grabbed the tire iron from Jake and loosened the lug nuts. He then handed the tire rod to Charles while he took off the tire and rolled it to the truck. He heaved the tire into the back of Charles' truck while

Jake got the spare from the back of the trailer. "I really appreciate you guys helping an old man out."

"Not a problem sir!" Rob said while lowering the jack and tightening up the lugs.

"I really wish I had some cash to give you."

"We wouldn't accept it anyway, if it were my dad on the side of the road I would want someone to stop and help him and Jake would want the same."

"Once you guys are done, why don't you come up to Fredericks Basin and have a cold beer with my sons and I."

" We would love to but I need to get back to town, we have had a long day and my girlfriend is waiting for us. She is already concerned we are coming back up here so I would hate to see her worrying any longer than she has too."

"What is she so concerned about?"

"Well it is a long story but since you are camping up here you should probably know." Rob and Jake then explained the entire story that had happened just the night before.

"Wow that is interesting, I saw a headline in the newspapers about something similar up Chapel Fork. I wonder if they are related, although that seems like a lot of ground for a bear to cover in only a few days."

"I don't know if it was the same animal or not but whatever it was sure scared us! Just make sure you are careful and watch for anything odd especially with your grandkids camping out." Rob said.

"Oh we will be, we will make sure everyone sleeps inside the trailers that way if a bear or mountain lion comes lurking around at night everyone is safe."

"Well I hope you have a fun and safe camping trip sir, come on Jake let's head up and grab your phone so we can go home."

"Thanks again for the help, it was nice meeting you. Have a safe drive."

Charles went back and climbed into his truck.

"That was sure nice of those boys to stop and help you change that tire out," Gloria said.

"Yes it was, it would have taken me a lot longer if it wasn't for their help."

Charles then started up his truck and headed down the road. He decided to keep the boy's story to himself so he didn't worry Gloria. Once he had pulled out Rob followed suit but instead of heading down the two lane highway they followed the turnoff to Aspen Grove. Once on this road they started up the five mile winding road that would lead to where they camped.

" Alright, we will have to hurry once we get up here or we aren't going to make it out before sunset."

"We will. I'm sure my phone is just lying on the ground, with its red case it should be easy to spot."

12

It was just about 6:30 when Charles & Gloria pulled into the campsite where George, Mike, and their families were waiting for them. They both gleefully waved and smiled as they pulled in. George and Mike walked up to the window and Mike said "Geez dad we thought you would be here hours ago we were starting to get worried!"

"I know I know we were running late as usual and then to top it off we blew a tire right by the Aspen Grove turn off."

"Glad to see you got the tire changed ok," George said

"Well I had some help, two boys that were headed up to Aspen Grove stopped and helped me change the tire."

"That was nice of them, were they headed up camping?" Mike asked.

"No, they had camped last night and one of them lost their phone."

"Wow, it must have been a wild party," Mike said with a laugh.

"Their story was a little different but I'm guessing it was a wild party!" Charles said with a smile.

"Ok dad, Mike and I will help you get set up and then we can start dinner. Mike, I will watch the driver's side if you watch the passenger side."

Mike gave a thumbs up and George started waving his hand telling Charles to back up. Charles slowly started backing up until George waved his hand telling him he had gone far enough.

After they were parked Gloria gave each of her sons a hug and told them she was glad to see them then she headed over to George's trailer where Maggie & Katrina were relaxing in their camp chairs and sipping on pina coladas.

"Hey girls it is so good to see you! Sorry we were late, it seemed like we just couldn't get our packing list marked off and then we blew a tire by Aspen Grove."

"Seems like quite an adventure! Glad you made it safely. It is great to see you as well," Maggie said.

"Now where are my grandkids? I can't wait to give all of them hugs."

" Clara and Marie are in the trailer playing UNO and the boys just headed off down the road on the four wheeler. I thought you might have seen them," Katrina said.

"No, they must have headed the other way. I guess I will have to get my hugs when they get back. GIRLS, GRANDMA is here!"

Both Marie and Clara came out of the trailer.

"GRANDMA" Marie yelled as she ran over to give Gloria a hug.

"Hi sweetie I've missed you. Have you been having fun today?"

"Yes, other than Joey pushing me into the river. It was freezing."

"Those wild boys" Gloria said as she walked over to Clara and gave her a hug."

"How are you darling? You are getting so tall and beautiful! I bet the boys are chasing you everywhere!"

Clara smiled. "Thanks Grandma, I'm doing well. I've just been enjoying the first week of summer break and hanging out with my friends."

"Alright I'm going to go into the trailer and chop up some potatoes for dinner," Maggie said.

"Oh why don't Katrina and I come in and help you. The guys won't have our trailer setup for a little bit."

They all headed into the trailer. Maggie, Gloria, & Katrina went to the kitchen table and Clara and Marie went to the bedroom to finish their game of UNO.

George went to the hitch of the trailer and started lowering the jack so they could unhook the trailer for Charles's truck. "Dad, why don't you give Mike your keys so he can grab the wheel blocks and we can get the trailer unhooked."

"Oh I can grab them, I'm not that old." Charles quipped. He then headed to the back of the trailer and opened up the storage bay while Mike followed. He handed Mike two wheel blocks and said "why don't you take care of the other side of the trailer and I will take care of this side."

They got the tires blocked so the trailer wouldn't roll and then Mike unhooked to the trailer.

"Dad, why don't you pull forward a little bit. We will need to lower the trailer to get you level." Charles jumped into the truck and pulled it for about four feet. They then lowered the front end of the trailer and got it level. "Alright Mike, why don't you lower the back stabilizer jacks while I lower the front ones," George said.

"Alright dad, anything else we need to help you with?"

"No George, I think I can get the rest of it. I just need to grab our chairs out of the back of the truck and I will be over.

"Ok I'm going to go over and start the coals so we can get the dutch oven potatoes cooking. It's already almost seven and they take about an hour to cook."

"I'm going to grab a few beers and I will meet you two over by the fire pit." Mike said.

George headed to his truck and grabbed a bag of charcoal and his dutch oven. He then went over to the fire pit and dumped some of the coals in his dutch oven chimney and sprayed them with lighter fluid. He let the fluid soak into the charcoal and then lit it with a match. After he made sure the charcoals had lit and would be ready he headed over to the trailer with the dutch oven. He opened the door and stuck his head in.

"Hey Maggie, are you ready for this dutch oven?"

"Yes I am thank you for bringing it to me. We are just in here catching up with your mom while cutting up the potatoes and onions. Do you want me to add some bacon to the potatoes?" she asked.

"Of course, it isn't a real batch of dutch oven potatoes without bacon is it?" he said with a smile.

" I will come back in a few minutes once the coals are hot, if you want to get it filled up and ready."

"Sounds great sweetie."

"Hey George, will you remind Mike that he needs to get the steaks out of the cooler and get them cooking?" Katrina asked.

"Yeah I will remind him."

"Thank you, he looks like he is getting pretty cozy in that chair of his."

George laughed and walked back toward where Charles and Mike were sitting.

"Hey Mike, Katrina wanted me to remind you that you need to get the steaks out of the cooler so you can get them ready to cook."

"I'm way ahead of her. I grabbed them out and put them in the trailer when I grabbed these beers. It's called efficiency" Mike said snarkly.

"Here is your beer brother."

The three of them sat in silence watching the hillside as the shadows started to cover the bottom of the canyon.

Steve & Joey were about five miles from camp headed up the canyon when Steve started to slow down and pulled off the side of the road near an old tree.

"What are we doing here?"

"I want to show you something really cool in this tree."

They got off the four wheeler and walked around to the other side of the tree and there was a big hole in it covered by a board.

"Wow what is this a cool hideout?"

Steve laughed. "No, it is an old storage area for fur trappers. They would leave supplies hidden in the tree so they could come back for them later."

"So like a hidden treasure map. That IS cool!"

"Yeah something like that, except instead of hiding coins and jewelry, they would hide their furs or food supplies for when they came back by this way they wouldn't have to carry everything".

Steve & Joey continued to look around by the tree and out to the west through a large field of wildflowers. After a few minutes they walked into the field and grabbed some wildflowers for their moms. While there weren't a lot that had bloomed yet there were a few to pick.

"Alright Joey you ready to head back to camp? We were told not to be gone very long."

"Can we go just a little bit further? I want to see if we can make it to the top of the mountain."

"Alright we can try to make it but we need to turn around in about fifteen minutes or we won't make it back before dark."

They jumped on the four wheeler and sped off down the road. Steve knew they wouldn't make it to the top of the mountain because it was about eight more miles and they needed to get back but he was having fun giving Joey a ride anyways.

They made it about three miles before Steve slowed the four wheeler down and told Joey that they needed to turn around. "Ah man, we are so close."

"I know but my dad will kick my butt if we aren't back before dark."

They turned around and headed back to camp. About a mile down the road Joey started yelling "STEVE STOP".

He slammed on the brakes. "What is it Joey?"

"Look over there"

There was a Cow moose and its calf walking through a beaver pond at the edge of the wildflower grove. They sat and watched them for a few minutes before the moose got nervous and headed through the wildflowers to a grove of Aspen.

"Alright Joey, now we really need to hurry. The sun is starting to set and we have about six miles to go."

As they started down the road again the sun was starting to dip behind the mountain tops and the wild flowers and trees were bathed in a beautiful orange glow from the sunset.

Steve & Joey entered into the pine trees after a few more miles and the air cooled down significantly. Steve shivered a little bit but knew they only had about two miles left in their journey. It had been an exciting first day of camping and they couldn't wait to get back to the campfire and have some dinner.

As they pulled into camp they could smell the dutch oven potatoes cooking and saw Grandpa Charles' truck and trailer. They pulled up next to George's truck and hopped off the four wheeler. Joey ran over to Charles was sitting.

"Grandpa!" He yelled as Charles stood up to give him a hug.

"How ya doin Joey? We have been waiting for you to get back."

Charles gave Joey a hug.

"You better go into the trailer and give your Grandma a hug she is excited to see you!"

"Hey Steve, how was your ride with Joey?" Charles said while giving him a hug.

"Hi Grandpa, it was good. We went to the trapper's cache tree and then tried to make it to the top of the mountain before dark but we ran out of time."

"Well it's a good thing you turned around, it gets cold once the sun goes down. Did you see any wildlife on your ride?"

"Yeah we saw a cow moose and her calf."

"Wow, where were you at?"

"They were in the beaver ponds that are just past the big wildflower field, about two miles past the trappers tree."

"That is pretty neat, Grandma wants to go up there and pick wildflowers at some point, maybe we will see them again when we go. You better follow Joey into the trailer and give your grandma a hug. I'm going to get a fire started now that dinner is about ready."

"George, does everyone in your family like their steaks cooked medium well?" Mike asked.

"Is there any other way to cook a steak?"

"HA no I don't believe so!"

"Hey dad, why don't you let me light the fire, it's going to be rough on your knees."

"Good lord George, I may be old but I'm not decrepit, I can light a fire."

"Alright, just offering to help."

"You can help by going and grabbing us three more beers from the cooler."

"Yes sir."

Steve and Joey went into Steve's family's trailer where Gloria was sitting and chatting with her two daughter in laws.

"My grandsons! How are you?"

"We are doing good Grandma."

"How was your four wheeler ride?"

"It was great, we picked these wildflowers for our moms and we saw a moose," Joey said as he handed his mom and Aunt Maggie the flowers.

"Awe thanks you two," Katrina said.

"I will grab us a few cups of water to place them in," Maggie said.

"That was sweet of you boys, where did you see the moose? I told your Grandpa on the way up I wanted to go find some wildflowers."

"We saw them just past the Trappers tree, if you know where that is."

"Oh that is wonderful that isn't too far, hopefully your Grandpa will take me for a ride this weekend and I can go pick some flowers."

"We can get you some tomorrow."

"Oh that is sweet of you Joey but I want to go for a ride anyway."

Just then George came over and told them that dinner was ready, they all headed outside to eat at the picnic table.

"Oh this looks and smells great! Thanks for cooking dinner tonight guys."

"No problem mom I just had to get the coals ready for the potatoes, Maggie, Katrina & Mike did most of the work."

They all sat down at the table with a plate full of dutch oven potatoes, green salad, and sirloin steaks. As they sat and ate their dinner they watched as the stars began to appear as the sky became darker. When they looked to the east, the Moon and Mars were rising.

13

Rob and Jake pulled into their campsite that they had just left this morning. They had about an hour until sunset and were hoping to find Jake's phone and be back onto the main highway by sunset. They both looked at each other and got out of the car to start searching for Jake's phone. They were both still spooked from the night before and the last thing they wanted to do was be stuck up here after dark. As they reached the front of the car it was decided that Rob would go and look around the campfire ring while Jake would go look around the trees where he was lying when he woke up earlier in the day.

Rob was looking around the fire pit for the phone when something caught his eye. "Hey Jake, were you walking around barefoot last night?"

"No, why?"

Rob contemplated what looked like the print of the front of a bare foot. "There is a print over here that I swear looks like the ball and toes of a foot but I can't tell."

Jake wandered over to where Rob was standing. He bent over to analyze the print that Rob was looking at.

"Yeah it does kind of look like a human footprint. Look right here though, it almost looks like there are claw markings right in front of the toes."

"You're right, I wonder what the hell it is?"

"My guess is these prints were here before we camped last night, I bet those are dog nail markings and someone happened to step right behind the paw print."

"I don't know, those claw marks look perfectly lined up with the toes."

"Yeah you're right I don't know what the hell it is. Come on, let's find my phone and get out of here, I was already spooked and this isn't helping."

Rob started walking toward where their tent and supplies had been set up in a small grove of aspen trees and Jake was retracing the path where he had been dragged through the brush during the attack.

After looking for another few minutes Rob was starting to get frustrated and nervous, he wanted to get out of the canyon soon. If they were to leave right now they would barely make it to the main road before it was completely dark.

"Hey Jake, I don't think we are going to find your phone man. We need to get back on the road real soon."

Jake didn't answer.

"Hey did you hear me?"

Still no answer. Rob started heading back towards where he found Jake earlier in the day. He saw Jake standing in almost the exact spot he had been lying, He looked to be in a trance staring off into the pine trees.

"Hey Jake are you ok?"

Jake acted as though he didn't hear him.

Rob ran over to Jake while looking into the trees trying to see what he was staring at. He grabbed his shoulder and shook him. "Hey man, are you ok?"

This startled Jake.

"Are you ok man?"

Jake looked over at him and pointed into the trees. About forty feet into the pines lay Jake's phone.

"Sweet you found your phone now let's go grab it and get the fuck out of here!" Rob started towards the phone but Jake grabbed his shoulder. "What are you doing? Let's get your damn phone and get the hell out of here.

"Look down," Jake said with a concerned look on his face. Rob looked down at the ground and leading into the trees were the footprints that they had seen near the firepit and as he looked into the tree he could see that there were a bunch of the same prints underneath the pines. "Awe shit! I left my gun in the car. Stay here I'm going to run and get it and then we will go grab your phone and get out of here."

Rob sprinted back to the car and grabbed his gun. When he looked back to where Jake was standing he was gone. He ran back to where Jake had been standing and there wasn't a sign of him. He looked on the ground for shoe prints and couldn't find any. He stared into the pine and realized Jake's phone was also gone.

"Jake, where did you go? This isn't funny your scaring the shit out of me?"

There was no response.

"Fuck man come on this is ridiculous you got your phone and it is going to be dark in like fifteen minutes let's get the hell out of here."

He turned on the flashlight on his phone and held it up with his left hand as he had his gun drawn in his right hand. As he slowly walked into the trees he could smell the strong scent of pine mixed with a pungent smell that could be best described as a dead animal. He was looking on the ground for any sign of Jake but all he saw were the strange footprints. He walked to the spot where Jake's phone had been sitting but there was no sign of it anywhere. He kept hoping that Jake was going to jump out from somewhere and try to scare him. But at the same time Jake had seemed stunned and in shock when Rob had decided to run back to the car and grab his gun. He doubted that Jake would now all of a sudden be in a joking mood.

He couldn't handle the stench any longer and went running out of the trees. He started walking around the edge of the pines trying to see if he could see any sign of Jake. Just as he got close to the dense shrub he heard something back in the pines.

"Jake, you pile of shit let's go, it is getting dark!"

Just as the last sunlight was shining on the tops of the trees Rob headed back into the pines to find Jake. He walked back into the pines about thirty feet from where he had last seen Jake.

"Come on you piece of shit. I'm leaving this is ridiculous! I helped you find your phone and now you are playing these games?"

He walked back over to where Jake's phone had been laying but still couldn't find any signs of Jake. He started heading out of the pines but stopped and turned around.

"Alright, I'm done with this bullshit. I'm going to go wait in the car. You have five minutes before I leave your ass up here."

"Jake, do you hear me?" he yelled.

He suddenly heard a snap from the tree above him and as he looked up all he could see was darkness. He started to point his flashlight towards the tops of the trees when all of a sudden he felt sickening pain on the back of his head. His gun was the first thing to hit the ground, followed by his phone and then Rob himself.

14

As the family finished up dinner it began to get chilly. Joey ran over to his trailer and grabbed his jacket as Charles grabbed a log and threw it in the fire to stoke it up. George & Mike were sitting back in their chairs and Maggie & Katrina along with Gloria headed into Maggie's trailer to finish up the dishes.

"Hey Steve, why don't you go grab the laser tag game and you four can play?" George said.

"I'm too full to run around right now," Clara said.

"Yeah me too, I think we should play Uno first," Marie chimed in.

"Alright let's play one round of Uno and then we can play laser tag," Steve said.

"Hey kids, why don't you play in Mike & Katrina's trailer since your Mom's are washing dishes in ours."

" Ok, I will go grab Uno out of our trailer and meet you & Clara at your trailer Marie."

The girls ran over to Mike's trailer just as Joey was coming out.

"Hey Joey we are going to play Uno, Steve just ran to grab the cards. Do you want to play?"

"I guess…. I'm glad I went and got my jacket to play laser tag," Joey said.

They all headed into the trailer and waited for Steve to get back.

"Hey mom, I'm just grabbing Uno so we can play while our bellies settle and then we are going to play laser tag."

"That sounds like a full night of fun!" Gloria said.

Steve smiled and went into the bedroom and grabbed the cards.

"See you in a little bit," he said as he took off out the door.

When he walked into the trailer the other kids were already sitting at the table waiting to play.

"Oh crap, I forgot to grab a drink!" Steve said.

"I will start dealing out the cards while you go grab your drink."

"Ok, you two watch her closely, Clara always tries to cheat me!"

Clara rolled her eyes and Steve laughed. He opened the door to the trailer and ran over to the cooler and grabbed a soda. When he got back into the trailer Clara was just finishing up dealing out the cards and was ready to begin the game.

"I wonder if those boys found their phone" Charles thought out loud.

"Hey boys I didn't want to say anything when the kids were around but did you see the headline about people being chased by some sort of animal up here?"

"I didn't see it but Maggie & the kids saw it while we were stopped at a gas station in Cherryton."

"Yeah I hadn't heard anything about it until George told me about it" Mike said.

"Do you think there is any merit to it?" Charles asked.

"I doubt it, there haven't been any predators bigger than a mountain lion seen up here in the last 20 years. I'm guessing the kids probably had a few too many drinks and one of their pals played a prank on them. Speaking of drinks, Dad or Mike do you want another beer?"

"I don't think either of us are going to pass that up!" Charles said.

" It's nothing to worry about, besides it was up Chapel Fork and that is at least 10 miles from here," Mike said.

"I'm sure you are right, just curious as to what it could have been. The boys that helped me fix my trailer said they had a similar encounter."

"I wouldn't worry too much about it Dad, I'm sure it's nothing. You know how people get weird about being in the wild if they aren't used to it."

"Yeah you are right George, I'm sure it's nothing."

George handed each of them a beer and then threw another log on the fire. As he sat down they heard the generator in the trailer kick on and soon a blender was running. A few minutes later Katrina, Gloria, & Maggie came out of the trailer carrying pina colada's. They each had two in their hands.

"Double fisting it tonight ladies?" Charles said with a laugh.

"Oh you know how we are Charles," Maggie said, chuckling.

"We were bringing each of you a drink but it looks like you already have that handled," Gloria said.

"Oh these beers? They are just about gone" Mike said as he got up and went to grab the ladies chairs to sit in.

They all handed their husbands a pina colada and sat down by the fire.

"Brrr. It's a little chilly for a frozen drink I guess isn't it?" Maggie said.

"Once you drink a few of those it will feel warmer," Charles said.

They all sat by the fire listening to the kids play Uno inside the trailer.

"It sure is a beautiful night," Katrina commented.

"Yeah it is, I love being able to see all the stars so brightly and would you look at that full moon!" Mike said.

"Hey George, how long do we have before you turn into a werewolf and start howling at the moon?" Mike asked.

"Ha! Maybe three more beers," George replied

"It was you that was chasing those kids around up here wasn't George?" Charles stated.

"What are you talking about?" Katrina asked.

Maggie rolled her eyes and then told Katrina and Gloria about the headline in the newspaper.

"I'm sure it was just kids playing pranks," George said.

They all sat quietly watching the fire and staring at the stars. The only noise that could be heard was from the river and from the kids playing Uno in the trailer.

15

It was just after eight in the evening when Becky woke up. She didn't realize she had even fallen asleep and was confused for a minute wondering if what had happened the night before and earlier in the day was just a dream. Once the brain fog had lifted she looked at the clock and wondered where Rob was.

The sun was beginning to set behind the western mountains in town but Becky knew from the night before that it was probably getting really dark up in the mountains. She looked at her phone and saw that Rob had texted her. "Hey sweetie, Officer Johnson called and talked to Jake for a little bit so we didn't get out of here as quickly as we wanted. I should be back to your apartment by nine or ten hopefully. I love you!" She looked at the time stamp and realized it was after just four when he sent it.

Those idiots! I hope they get out of there before dark, I don't want them wandering around the woods with whatever tried to kill Jake, she thought.

She got up and paced for a few minutes scrolling Instagram and Facebook. She then went to the kitchen where she stared out her window looking at the eastern mountain range knowing Rob and Jake may still be out there.

 She figured that sitting there and worrying wouldn't solve anything she poured herself a glass of wine and went back to the living room to turn the TV on. While flipping through the channels she realized she was lost in thought and hadn't even been watching as the channel menu crossed the screen. She finally flipped the channel over to ABC where *The Bachelor* finale was on. It wasn't her favorite show but maybe the drama on the tv would pull her away from worrying about Rob & Jake. Becky then grabbed her phone and sent a text to Rob asking him to please call or text her as soon as he got service to let her know he was ok.

Up in the canyon the Jacob's family was sitting around the fire when Charles got up out of his chair.

"Well I guess I will hit the hay. Morning will be here before you know it," Charles said.

"Already dad? It's barely ten."

"Hey that coffee pot will be calling my name by 6am, and I gotta get my beauty sleep," They all laughed and rolled their eyes at Charles.

Charles stood up and asked "Are you coming with me Gloria?"

"No, I think I will stay up for a bit and watch the kids play for a little while longer. It's not often that I get to sit and enjoy all of their giggles anymore."

Charles had continued his early morning schedule after retiring from the railroad five years before. He was always up by 5:30 in the morning and usually in bed by ten at night.

"Alright I will see you in a little while."

He bent over and kissed Gloria good night and then told the kids to pause their laser tag game and come and give him a hug.

"Goodnight Grandpa," they all said as they each gave him a hug.

"Kids, I think it's about time to go to bed," Maggie said.

"Oh come on mom we are tied and need to finish this round to see if the boy or girls are the champions."

They had been playing laser tag for the last hour or so but the last two rounds had been boys against girls and each team had won a round so they needed the additional round to see who the winners were.

"Alright fine one more round or 10:30 whichever comes first then it is off to bed without any arguments."

"Thanks mom! Let's get back to our game," Steve yelled.

Each team headed back to their main bases which were groups of trees on each side of camp. Normally the kids would play laser tag further into the tree line but their parents told them to stay where they could see them this time. While Joey never would admit it he was glad Uncle George had made that request because he was a little nervous after the story he had heard from Steve.

"WAHOO WE ARE THE CHAMPIONS" Steve yelled.

He had just shot his sister for her final death of the round. He had just knocked Marie out of the game a few seconds before. "Dang Steve you are a good shot!" Joey said.

All four of them wandered back over to the campfire where their parents were sitting.

"Are you all done playing?" Maggie asked.

"Yeah mom we are done. Guess what, we are the champions!"

"I heard, in fact I think the whole canyon knows you won." she said with a laugh.

"Alright you two head in and brush your teeth and get in bed, Dad and I will be in shortly."

Steve and Clara gave everyone a hug and headed into the trailer.

"I get to brush my teeth first." Steve said.

His sister always took forever washing her face and brushing her teeth so he hated waiting on her.

Steve finished brushing his teeth and crawled up onto the bunk bed where he slept. He grabbed his tablet and started playing a game on it while he waited for Clara to brush her teeth and wash her makeup off. After about ten minutes she came out and folded the couch into a bed. "The least you could have done is pulled my bed out while I was brushing my teeth you dirtbag."

"What was that you wanted me to tell mom you were calling names so you can be grounded from your phone?"

"Shut it Steve, you know I was just teasing you. Now put your tablet away and I will turn off the light."

Steve turned his tablet off and laid there in bed. His mind wandered to the story he had read in the newspaper and tried to imagine what had happened in his head. He was pretending to be a detective and working out the details of the attack and what it could have been. Soon his eyes began to get heavy and he drifted off to sleep.

Over in Mike & Katrina's trailer Joey and Marie had brushed their teeth and laid down in their beds. Marie slept on the table that turned into a bed and Joey slept on the couch. Katrina had made their beds up earlier in the night while dinner was cooking.

Out by the fire it was quiet, everyone was sipping the last of their drinks and watching the flames of the fire die down.

"Do any of you have the eerie feeling that someone is watching us right now?" Maggie asked.

"Ha! It's probably the kids peeking out the window at us" Mike said.

"Yeah I feel it too. It feels like someone or something is on the mountain side watching us," Katrina said.

Mike grabbed his flashlight and pointed it up on the mountain side, well as far as it would go anyway. There wasn't anything close to camp.

"It may be a moose or cows up on the hillside. I'm sure you are just feeling a little uneasy about the story in the newspaper."

"Yeah you're probably right, I know there is nothing to worry about sometimes the darkness in the mountains just creeps me out a little bit," Maggie said.

They all sat around the fire for a few more minutes before they all started to trickle one by one into their trailers for the night. First Gloria headed to her trailer and with Charles snoring it sounded like a Grizzly bear had taken up residence.

Katrina was next to go check on the kids and make sure they had gotten inside their sleeping bags. Her kids were known for falling asleep outside the sleeping bag and with as cold as it already felt she wanted them bundled up so they didn't wake her and Mike up in the middle of the night.

Finally Maggie decided it was bedtime, she gave George a kiss and headed towards the trailer. When she opened the door Clara was still up reading a book on her kindle.

"Hey sweetie, how is it going?"

"Fine, I've just been reading my book."

She turned it off and laid it next to her.

"Mom, do you think the story in the newspaper might actually be true? I kept getting a weird feeling that something was watching us while we were playing laser tag."

"It may be true but I really don't think there is anything to worry about. It happened a long way from here and there aren't many bears, if any up this canyon."

"What about the feeling that something was watching us?"

"There could have been something watching you, there are moose up here as well as all of the cows we have seen. I'm sure it isn't anything to worry about, now get some rest." Maggie kissed Clara on the forehead and headed for the bedroom. She knew how Clara felt but also knew how small the chances of being attacked by a wild animal in this area was.

Out by the fire Mike and George sat talking about their jobs and how nice it was to get away from work for a little while.

"You want another beer?" Mike asked.

"I think I'm done for the night," George said.

"Oh come on you can have one more" Mike said as he opened up the can and handed it to George. They both sat back in their chairs enjoying the brisk air and watching the flames of the dying fire. After looking up at the stars for a few minutes Mike looked over at his brother. He was glad they were able to get away like this and enjoy camping as a family. They didn't get to see each other often so times like these were priceless.

FRIDAY

16

It was just after midnight and Becky was starting to get really worried, she still hadn't heard from Rob. She had called his and Jake's phone multiple times but wasn't getting an answer. At first she had assumed that they were just running late but now she was starting to get really worried.

Becky didn't know whom to call, she thought about calling her parents or Rob's parents but there wouldn't be much they could do other than worry since they were two hundred miles away. She then thought about calling her best friend Kate to see if she would go with her up the canyon to see if they could find Rob & Jake but she also knew that Kate had to work the next day and she didn't want to bother her.

As she was standing at the kitchen counter she looked over at the table and realized that she had Officer Johnson's card on the table. She walked over to the table to see what phone numbers were on the card. On the front it had his name and rank as well as his email and desk phone number. She flipped the card over and realized he had written his cell phone number as well as the case number on the card.

Becky walked into the living room and grabbed her phone, she dialed Office Johnson's number and the phone began to ring. After four rings his phone went to voicemail. Becky sighed and thought to herself " Of course he isn't going to answer, he was on duty all day and probably has to work tomorrow."

As Becky was sitting at the table trying to think of what to do next her phone began to ring, it was Officer Johnson.

She answered, "Officer Johnson?"

"Yes this is him, who is this?" he asked in a groggy voice.

"Officer Johnson this is Becky, I met with you earlier this morning about my friend Jake being attacked by some sort of animal last night."

"Yes Becky I remember you what is going on?"

"Rob & Jake went back up the canyon this evening to try and find Jake's phone. I'm getting..."

"Wait what, they went back up the canyon? I spoke with Jake this afternoon around four and he didn't mention anything about it."

"Yeah Jake was worried his dad would be mad if he called and told him he lost his phone so they went back up the canyon to try and find it. I'm getting really worried because Rob told me he would be home by ten and it is after midnight. I would have thought Jake would have mentioned it to you when you talked to him."

"He didn't mention it. Give me a few minutes. I'm going to call the Game Warden who was assigned this case and see what we should do."

"How long is it going to take? I'm ready to drive up the canyon and look for them myself!"

"Becky there is no reason for you to head up the canyon, it's dangerous at night. There are a lot of deer and other wildlife roaming around this time of year that you could easily hit. If we have to respond to a wreck that you are involved in it takes away from us finding out where Rob and Jake are. I will call dispatch and make sure there haven't been any wrecks reported and then I will call you. Once I have done that I will call the Game Warden and figure out what we are going to do. Does that sound good?"

"Ok"

"Give me five minutes to call dispatch and then we will talk again."

"Ok, bye" Becky said with a very concerned tone in her voice.

Terry hung up the phone and sighed. He walked into the bathroom and took a piss, when he came back his wife Joselyn was sitting up in bed.

"Hey honey, what's going on?"

He told her about the case and how Becky was worried about Rob & Jake. He told her he was going to make a few calls and for her to go back to sleep. Terry then grabbed his phone off of the nightstand and walked into the kitchen. He grabbed a glass of water hoping that it would help wake him up so he sounded coherent when he called dispatch. He then sat down at the kitchen table and dialed the number for the dispatch officer working the night shift.

"Cherryton City dispatch, this is Janice speaking how can I help you."

Terry was glad to hear Janice's voice. She was a good friend of his who had been working dispatch for over twenty years.

"Hi Janice, this is Terry Johnson, how are you?"

"I'm doing good dear what are you doing up at this hour? You have to be on shift at seven."

"I know but I got a call tonight from a girl that I have been working a case on. It has to do with the kids that claimed they were chased last night by some sort of creature. Anyway her boyfriend and his friend aren't home yet and she is really worried. Have there been any wrecks up Cherryton Canyon tonight?"

"No, it has been a fairly quiet night, nothing out of the norm."

"Ok thanks,I'm going to call Gabe Campbell and just make sure Fish & Game hasn't heard anything and then I'm going back to bed."

"Ok dear, tell Joselyn hi for me and get some rest. It's summer and tomorrow's Friday so I'm sure it is going to be a busy day!"

"Thank Janice, talk to you later."

Terry hung up his phone and put his head in his hands, while he was glad that the boys hadn't been in a wreck this would mean he would be up even longer before he went back to sleep and as Janice had said tomorrow was sure to be a busy day. He mustered up some energy and dialed Becky's number.

Becky paced her living room floor looking at the screen on her phone and waiting for it to ring. After what seemed like an hour, it started to buzz. She answered immediately,

"Hello."

"Hi Becky. I just got off of the phone with dispatch and the good news is there haven't been any wrecks up the canyon."

"What is the bad news?"

"Well I don't have any bad news, I just don't have answers. I'm going to call Gabe Campbell who is the Fish & Game officer taking over this case and see if there have been any calls to their office tonight."

Terry hung up the phone and found Gabe's contact on his phone. He and Gabe had gone to High School together and were good friends. He clicked on Gabe's contact and pressed call. The phone rang a few times without an answer. Soon Gabe's voicemail picked up.

"Hey Gabe, it's Terry. I just had a question on the case I had referred over to you yesterday. Becky called me a few minutes ago because her boyfriend Rob and his friend Jake went back up the canyon and haven't returned home. Anyways give me a call when you receive this, thanks."

Gabe was probably asleep. The summer weekends were Gabe's busiest time of the year next to hunting season.

Terry figured he would give it ten minutes and then call Becky back. If dispatch hadn't heard anything and Gabe wasn't out on a call he assumed everything was fine and the boys just hadn't made it back yet.

He sat thinking about how tired he was going to be tomorrow. He rested his head on the table and stared at the clock. It was now almost 12:45 and he would need to be up in four and a half hours if he wanted to get his workout in before his shift. Five minutes went by and Terry was starting to doze off when his phone started ringing. He looked at the caller id and it was Gabe.

"Morning Gabe, did you get my voicemail?"

"I guess you can call it morning, yes I got your voicemail. I haven't received any calls from dispatch here or up in Bear Lake. Do you think there is something we need to investigate or do you think the boys are just not home yet?"

"My brain tells me there is nothing to worry about. They probably got home late and Rob didn't call Becky before he fell asleep. My gut tells me something weird is going on up the canyon, I'm just not sure which is correct yet."

Gabe sighed, "Alright I will be over in about an hour and we can head up the canyon."

He knew Terry too well to believe that he was just going to go back to sleep."

"No, let's leave it until morning, I'm sure they just went home and fell asleep."

"Alright I will head up the canyon first thing in the morning around and checkout Aspen Grove and give you a call, it will probably be around six by the time I investigate and get back to an area with service."

"Ok I will talk to you then, I'm going to call Becky back and let her know what I've found out."

After the call was over Terry went to his recent calls and redialed Becky's number.

"Hello"

"Hi Becky, it's Terry. I just got off the phone with Gabe Campbell and he said that his office hadn't received any reports of anything suspicious going on up the canyon. Do you think that Rob & Jake made it home and Rob happened to fall asleep before he had a chance to call you back?"

"No, he knew how worried I was. He would have made sure to at least text me when they got home. What do we do next?"

"Well Gabe is going to go up to Aspen Grove first thing in the morning and see if they happen to still be there and then he will update me."

"First thing in the morning? So I'm just supposed to sit around and wait until morning to figure out what happened? That isn't going to work, I'm heading up there right now."

"Look I can't stop you but it is already one in the morning, Gabe will be leaving his house at five and I should have heard from him by seven at the latest. Please just try and get some sleep and I will call you as soon as I find anything out."

Becky sighed, "I better get a call first thing in the morning."

"As soon as I hear anything I will let you know."

Becky hung up the phone, irritated with the whole situation. Her boyfriend was missing and no one seemed to care. She decided to drive past Rob's apartment to see if his car was there.

Maybe he did just fall asleep and forget to call, she thought.

She grabbed her car keys and headed out the door. As she drove down the dark deserted streets she really hoped she would see Rob's car, if she did she would be able to go home and go back to sleep without worrying.

She pulled into the parking lot entrance closest to Rob's apartment and looked at the spot where he normally parked, but it was empty. Becky then decided to drive around the entire complex to make sure he didn't park somewhere else, every once in a while someone would park in his spot and he would have to find somewhere else to park.

She made her way around the entire parking lot without finding Rob's car.

She thought to herself, "Maybe I missed it. I'm going to go knock on the door and see if they answer."

While getting out of the car and heading to Rob's apartment door she had a feeling this was going to end very badly. She went up to the door and knocked but no one answered. She pulled out her phone and called both Rob & Jake but neither answered their phones and she couldn't hear them ringing inside the apartment either. She walked back to the car and tears began to stream down her face. She didn't know what to do. She climbed into her car, started it up and tried to pull herself together. After a few minutes she made the decision that there was no way she was going to be able to sleep so she headed up the canyon.

It was just after 2 am as Becky turned on to the Aspen Grove turn off. She had only passed three cars the entire way up the canyon and hadn't seen Rob's car anywhere. Her hope now was that she would get to the campsite and Rob & Jake would be asleep in the car.

She continued up the winding road slowly making sure she didn't see Rob's car off of the road on one of the bends. When she finally got to the camp spot she pulled off the road and her headlights reflected brightly off the passenger side of Rob's car. She didn't see movement in the car and no one was in the front seats. Her heart began to race, she slammed the car into park and jumped out.

"ROB" she yelled twice but never heard a reply.

She ran over to his car and realized that the door was unlocked. Now she really knew something was wrong. Rob never left his car unlocked.

"ROB" she yelled again.

Still no response. She went back to her car and grabbed the large flashlight her father had given her for Christmas. After grabbing the flashlight she started looking around worried for not only Rob & Jake's safety but her own. She tried to keep her fear at bay and decided she was going to find out what had happened as she slowly started walking back towards the car she was shining her flashlight around to hopefully keep any animals away but to also see if she could see any signs of Rob.

She made it back to Rob's car and looked around inside. There wasn't anything out of place so she sat down in the driver's seat and turned on the headlights so she had more light. When the lights came on she looked out the windshield and could see the light reflecting off of something laying on the ground near the pine trees.

Becky got out of the car and started to slowly walk towards the pines.

"ROB" she called again.

She reached the item that was reflecting light and realized it was a gun. It looked just like the gun Rob owned. She pointed the flashlight into the pines but didn't see anything. She then picked up the gun and ran back to her car not knowing what to do next. She jumped into the driver's seat and locked the doors.

There was no longer any question, something horrible had happened and she needed to get help. She started her car, put it in reverse and turned around. As she put the car in drive she slammed on the accelerator and started racing down the road. As she came around a corner, halfway to the highway, her headlights shined onto a doe and fawn crossing the road. She slammed on her brakes and swerved to the left missing the deer but careening off the side of the road. The last thing she remembered was seeing a tree coming directly at her before her airbag went off.

Becky awoke after a few minutes choking on the powder from her airbag dazed and with a sharp pain in the middle of her face and blood running down over her lips from her nose. While the airbag saved her life her nose had been broken by the force of impact.

After realizing what had happened she thought to herself "Could this night get any worse?"

She reached over for her phone but it was no longer on the seat and neither was Rob's gun. After unbuckling from her seatbelt she tried to reach over to feel if she could find her phone on the floor but the pain in her ribs was so intense she screamed in agony and rested against her seat.

"My ribs must be broken," she thought.

The only thing she could hear was the hiss of the steam leaking from the radiator. She then tried to open the car door but it was jammed and with her broken ribs she couldn't muster the energy to push it open.

"Now what am I going to do?"

It was around three in the morning and she knew the road probably wouldn't have any traffic on it until at least five or six when people trying to get an early start fishing would start driving up the road. As she sat there trying to figure out what to do she looked to her right and thought she saw something moving in the trees.

"What was that? Am I seeing things?" she thought to herself.

Soon she noticed the movement again. Now she began to get very worried, she couldn't get out of the car. She decided her best bet was to try and reach the gun again. Although she had only fired it once, Rob had taught her how to load and fire the gun. Becky knew that reaching the gun may be her only chance at survival.

She leaned over to the passenger seat attempting to find the gun, pain radiating through her left side. Still she reached to the floor and tried to feel the gun, as reached further under the dash she felt the butt of the gun. She grabbed it, feeling the cold steel in her hands as laid there trying to recompose herself.

Becky tried to sit up but it was too painful so she lay there waiting to see what was moving in the trees. She knew she would have to sit up in order to give herself a fighting chance of shooting whatever was out there. As she sat up she could feel the broken pieces of her rib moving.

She was able to get to a sitting position and looked out the driver's side window. In the trees she saw a large animal moving around. Becky lifted the gun and shot two times and whatever was moving in the tree line took off running. Becky began to feel lightheaded and this time instead of the feeling going away her vision began to fade even more after a few more seconds Becky passed out. The gun slid between the door and the seat.

17

It was just after 4am when Gabe rolled out of bed. He didn't get much sleep after he got off of the phone with Terry. He walked into the bathroom, took a piss and brushed his teeth and hair. He then wandered into the kitchen and poured himself a cup of black coffee. The remaining coffee he placed in his coffee mug and his thermos. He knew he would need the extra caffeine today.

Gabe put some bread into the toaster and cracked an egg into the frying pan. While these were cooking he went and put on his uniform. He came back into the kitchen and flipped the egg. He enjoyed an over-easy egg spread on top of his toast.

Gabe sat down at the kitchen table eating his breakfast and sipping on his coffee. He thought about what possibly could be causing all of the havoc up in the canyon. He had only seen a black bear twice in the ten years that he had been working as a game warden and they were normally very skittish animals. If there was a black bear chasing people around the forest he was worried that it may have rabies.

Gabe finished his breakfast and rinsed off his plate and guzzled down his coffee. He grabbed his lunch box, coffee mug, & thermos and headed out the door.

There was a cool breeze blowing as he unlocked his truck and loaded his things into the back seat. He jumped into the driver's seat and started up his truck. He looked at the clock which read 4:53am. Then he turned on his radio and called into dispatch letting them know he was on duty. He backed out of the driveway and headed down the road towards main street. As he drove down main street it was a quiet Friday morning. He made a left hand turn on to 4th South and headed east towards the mountains. He made this drive almost every day during the summer where his routine was to drive the highway all the way to Bear Lake while looking for roadkill to clean up before the road got busy.

Today he would make the same drive but would make a detour up to Aspen Grove before heading to Bear Lake. He assumed that nothing would be out of the ordinary but he wanted to check so when he was at the top of the canyon he could call Terry and let him know what he found.

It took Gabe roughly thirty minutes to get to the Aspen Grove turnout. It had been an uneventful drive with very little traffic. He knew that would start changing shortly as fisherman and campers started heading up the canyon for the weekend.

Gabe turned off at the highway onto the Aspen Grove road and headed up the hill. As the sun slowly started to light the sky he could tell it was going to be a beautiful day. He eased up the road looking to see if there was any wildlife moving around. This was one of the best times to see animals as they were usually our grazing. He drove up the road and as he was rounding one of the curves he noticed there was a car off the side of the road and it looked like the driver was unconscious.

Gabe slammed on his brakes and flipped the switch to his emergency lights and threw the truck in park. He jumped out the door, running over to the car "Are you alright?" he yelled. There was no response, he felt for a pulse and watched the driver's chest. Her breathing was shallow and she had a faint pulse. He ran back to his truck and grabbed the emt bag he carried in his back seat. He reached into the front seat and grabbed his radio so he could call for an ambulance and back up. He knew that the road would be getting busier as the morning went on and he would need help.

"Dispatch this is GW139 do you copy?"

"GW139 we copy, go ahead"

"Dispatch I have an 11-80 on the Aspen Grove road approximately three miles from the turnoff. Send medical and backup for traffic control."

"GW139 copy 11-80 on Aspen Grove road approximately three miles from the turnoff. I am dispatching medical and assistance for traffic control."

Gabe ran back over to the car and checked on the injured driver, she was still breathing albeit with a struggle. He wanted to try and leave her in the car until he had assistance in case she had a back or neck injury.

He called back to dispatch "Dispatch can I get a 10-28 on this license plate so we can try to identify the driver?"

"10-4 GW139 what is the license plate number?" Gabe read them the license plate and waited for a response."

"GW139 this car is registered to Becky Robinson."

Immediately Gabe's thoughts went to his discussion earlier in the morning with Terry. This had to be the Becky that Terry had been speaking with, it was too much of a coincidence.

Thirty miles away Terry's alarm clock was going off for the second time. After getting off the phone with Gabe & Becky he had a hard time getting back to sleep. Terry reached over and turned his alarm clock off. He then sat there for a few minutes thinking to himself

Gabe should be getting to Aspen Grove here shortly. Hopefully he hasn't found anything, he thought

Terry put on his workout clothes and went and used the restroom. Then he went into the kitchen to grab a cup of coffee. After sitting and drinking his coffee and scrolling through Facebook for a few minutes he grabbed a water bottle and headed towards his basement gym. Terry knew being a police officer could be dangerous and being in the best shape possible was an advantage. It was now 5:40 and Terry figured he would run for 20 minutes on the treadmill and await the call from Gabe.

At the same time that Terry was climbing on to the treadmill Gabe could hear the sirens from the emergency service vehicles headed up the road. The first vehicle he saw was a Sheriff's deputy for Cassia county.

"Hey Jim, will you go up the road and stop traffic before it starts down the hill?"

Jim nodded his head and sped off up the hill.

Just behind Jim the ambulance and fire teams pulled up. Gabe walked over to them to give them a status update as they grabbed their equipment. He told them Becky's health status and let them get to work. The paramedics went up to the car and tried to wake Becky but there was no response. Based on her broken nose and swollen face they were worried about swelling in her brain. From what they could see Becky didn't have her seatbelt on when the wreck occurred and when her airbag went off it slammed her into the driver's side window which had caused a large laceration on the side of her head.

Jill, the lead paramedic, stabilized Becky's neck and had her crew grab a backboard so they could place her on it. They took her vitals, her heart beat and blood pressure were low. Jill was worried that Becky may have an internal bleed due to her low blood pressure. She wanted to get her to the hospital as soon as possible. They slowly pulled Becky out of the car and lowered her onto the backboard. They then placed her on a stretcher and wheeled her to the ambulance. Gabe followed them to the ambulance and helped load her in. He then watched as they placed an IV in her arm and an oxygen mask over her face. After a few minutes they confirmed her vitals although low were stable. Jill stayed in the back while one of the other paramedics jumped into the driver's seat. Jill looked at him and said she is lucky she had a coat on or she probably would have frozen to death. She is also lucky you came along when you did Gabe or she wouldn't have a chance of survival. Gabe closed the doors to the back of the ambulance and it pulled away with the sirens blaring.

After the ambulance left Gabe looked over at the car. Fred, one of the Sheriff's deputies, was taking pictures, he would be leading the investigation into how the wreck occurred. Gabe already knew what more than likely had happened. Becky would have been driving down the road late at night and there were always deer crossing the road. He could picture it in his head the deer would have been walking across the roadway and she swerved to miss the deer causing herself and her car way more damage than if she would have just hit the animal. Gabe decided he better call dispatch and have them get a hold of Terry since he knew Terry was expecting a call at six and it was already almost seven. His guess was it would be well after eight before they got this mess cleaned up and traffic flowing again.

It was just after six when Terry climbed off of the treadmill. He decided that it may take Gabe a little longer to get a hold of him if he got held up in the canyon for any reason so he grabbed his phone and went to the bathroom. He placed his phone on the bathroom sink, undressed, and climbed into the shower. He sat with the hot water running over his body and just tried to enjoy the peace and quiet before his busy day. After getting out of the shower Terry dried off and checked his phone. He hadn't missed any calls or texts so he assumed Gabe was running late. He walked back into the kitchen to cook an omelet for breakfast and poured himself another cup of coffee. He grabbed a bowl out of the cupboard and the eggs out of the fridge. Just as he was cracking the first egg into the bowl his phone began to ring. He grabbed his phone out of his pocket and was expecting to see Gabe's name on the caller id. The number he saw was from the office was not from Gabe. He answered the phone "Officer Johnson speaking."

"Terry, it's Shelly." Shelly was the dispatch officer who took over for Janice at 6am. "Hey Shelly, how is it going?"

"It's too early to tell yet I will let you know in a few hours" she said with a laugh. "Hey I was calling you because Gabe Campbell with Fish and Game called me and wanted me to relay a message to you."

"Ok what is it, I was expecting a call from him around six. Is everything alright?"

"Everything is fine with him, but he wanted to let me know that a girl you had been working with on a case was in an accident this morning up the road to Aspen Grove."

"Shit" Terry mumbled under his breath.

"Is she ok?"

"They are in the process of transferring her to the hospital right now. Gabe said she had a broken nose, a head laceration and possibly a brain injury. She was unresponsive when the ambulance left."

"I told her to stay home and we would look for Rob & Jake this morning. Did Gabe mention anything about those two?"

"No he didn't, do I need to put a bulletin out to be on the lookout for something?"

"No not yet. Thanks for the head's up. Let me know if you hear anything else and I will be in the office by eight."

"Ok we will see you then."

Terry all of a sudden wasn't hungry, he was hoping that Becky would have waited till this morning to go look for Rob & Jake. This was exactly what he was worried about, not only was Becky now fighting for her life but if the boys were truly missing the only other witness to the events from the night before now couldn't speak.

As he was sitting at the table sipping on his coffee his wife walked into the kitchen. "Is everything alright?"

"No, Becky, the girl I was talking to about the incidents up the canyon was involved in a car wreck up Aspen Grove."

"Oh no, is she ok? What was she doing going up there in the middle of the night?"

"Well I assume she went looking for her boyfriend and wrecked while either going up or coming down the canyon. I didn't get many details from Shelly. She did say she is hurt pretty bad and they are bringing her into the hospital. I'm going to head over there right now and see what I can find out."

"Do you want me to finish making your breakfast first?"

"No you can have it, I'm not hungry anymore"

Terry walked into the bedroom and got dressed. He was finishing tightening his belt as he walked into the kitchen.

"Here, I made you a breakfast burrito and poured you some coffee. You have to eat if you are going to be on patrol all day."

"Thank sweetie."

He gave Joselyn a kiss and hug goodbye and headed out the door. Terry climbed into his police cruiser, turned his car and radio on. He then decided he would call Shelly instead of radioing in.

"Hey Shelly, it's Terry. I'm going to be 10-8 the (code for on shift) but as long as I'm not immediately needed anywhere I'm going to head to the hospital and see what I can find out about Becky."

"Ok I will put you 10-8 at 7:53 and enroute to the hospital for an investigation."

"Thanks Shelly."

Terry backed out of his driveway and headed to the hospital. He didn't know if he would get any information from the hospital but he was hoping to at least find out Becky's status. He was regretting not going out last night and trying to investigate. Maybe Becky wouldn't have headed up the canyon if he had done that.

18

It was just after 6:30 up Fredericks Basin and the sun was just starting to come over the hillside. Charles climbed out of his trailer with a coffee mug in hand, steam rising into the brisk air. Charles loved this time of morning up in the mountains. The only thing out moving was the animals. The birds were beginning to chirp in the trees and Charles could see a few cows up on the hillside grazing. Charles grabbed his camping chair and sat down in the morning sun as it slowly creeped across the valley. He knew soon the entire family would be up and they would be entertained by the kids, but for now he was content just enjoying the peaceful morning.

About fifteen minutes later George came out of his trailer carrying his coffee mug.

"Morning dad, how did you sleep?"

"Like a baby, how about you?"

"I slept well, but my head hurts a little this morning. Probably too many drinks last night but don't tell Maggie" he said with a chuckle.

They both were sitting around in silence enjoying the morning sun when the door to George's trailer opened and out came Steve and Maggie.

"Morning you two. How did you sleep?" Charles said.

"Good" Steve said as he was rubbing his eyes and drinking hot chocolate. Maggie walked over and grabbed them both chairs and sat down next to George.

"Morning sweetie, when do you want us to start breakfast?" George asked.

"Oh we can wait 30 minutes or so I think, I know Mike and Katrina will want to sleep in and Clara is getting her beauty sleep."

"Yeah you don't want to wake the teenage beast!" Steve replied.

"Be nice to your sister, she isn't even out here to defend herself," Maggie said.

A little after seven Gloria came out of the trailer.

"Charlie, have you started breakfast?"

"Good morning to you as well dear."

"I don't want everyone to be hungry."

"I will get the griddle out and get it heating up if you go and mix up the pancake batter." Gloria shut the door and went to find the pancake mix.

"Well everyone I have my marching orders I better get going." Charles said.

"George, do you want me to go get the bacon out of the trailer so we can get it cooking?" Maggie asked.

"Yeah that would be great. I will go help Dad get the griddle set up."

Steve asked if he could walk down to the river and see if he could see any fish. George told him to go ahead but to stay out of the water. It was too cold to be getting wet this early in the day.

Steve slowly wandered down to the river. It wasn't far from camp but he was on his own and a little nervous. In the back of his mind he was worried that whatever had been chasing people may have moved over to this canyon. As he got down to the edge of the river he could see a few fish swimming in the deeper pools.

Joey & I will have to try and catch a few later on, he thought.

They usually didn't have much luck catching the fish in the river but it was a good way to pass the time. He sat down on the edge of the river and looked around and then as most little boys do he started trying to skip rocks across the water. He was looking up at the hillside when he heard something rustle in the brush behind him. He quickly turned around but didn't see anything. After the headlines in the newspaper and being spooked while out on the trail with Joey yesterday he decided he didn't want to be alone and headed back to camp for breakfast. As he walked into camp it seemed like everyone must have woken up at the same time. George and Mike were watching the bacon as Maggie and Katrina cut up the fruit. Over at his grandparents trailer Charles & Gloria were pouring pancake batter on to the griddle.

"Good morning Steve, where is Joey?" Marie asked.

"Good morning, I don't know I haven't seen him."

"He said he was going to go down to the river and see if he could find you, didn't you see him?"

"No I didn't see him, I wonder if he went to a different spot."

"Mom, can Steve & I go try and find Joey?"

"He didn't find you Steve? He followed the path that you went down."

"No I didn't see him, we will go look for him."

"Steve be back in ten minutes no matter what, we don't need all three of you missing and he probably wandered down to a different spot on the river where the trail splits."

"Ok uncle Mike we will be back."

As they started down the trail Joey was on the other end petrified. He had heard something move through the brush but all he could see was a large dark shadow. He was afraid that it might be a moose and if he were to startle it the animal would charge him. Joey slowly backed down the bank of the river thinking that if the moose charged him he would jump into the river and hope that the moose wouldn't follow him. He suddenly heard Steve & Marie's voice coming down the trail and the beast started to move in the brush. He didn't know what to do, he didn't want Steve and Marie to get attacked by whatever was in the brush.

"STEVE, MARIE. I'M DOWN HERE BY THE RIVER STAY BACK THERE IS SOMETHING IN THE BRUSH."

Steve and Marie stopped in their tracks.

"Marie go grab our dad's. I'm going to see what is in the brush."

Marie turned around and started running down the trail and Steve slowly continued down toward Steve. Suddenly he heard the brush begin to rustle and shake and whatever had been in the brush took off up the river bank. Steve then ran down the trail to the riverbank where Joey was standing.

"What was that?" Steve asked.

"I'm not sure I couldn't get a good look, but whatever it was it was big!" Joey said.

"Let's get back to camp, breakfast is almost ready."

As they were about halfway down the trail, Mike and George were running towards them.

"Steve & Joey, What is going on? Marie is scared out of her mind!" Mike said.

"I don't know what it was Dad, I was down by the river and heard some rustling in the brush and when I looked over there was a big dark animal standing in the brush but I couldn't tell what it was. I backed down to the river thinking it might be an ornery moose and that is when I heard Steve and Marie."

"I told Marie to run back to camp, Uncle Mike. I didn't want to leave Joey alone."

"Did you get a good look at the animal Joey?"

"No the brush was too thick so I couldn't tell what it actually was and it ran off when it heard Steve."

"Alright well let's get back to camp, from now on you guys need to travel in pairs, you shouldn't be going out on your own in the woods," Mike replied.

They walked back to camp. As they got closer they caught the scent of bacon and couldn't wait for breakfast.

"Is everything alright?" Katrina asked.

"Yes everything is alright, there was something in the brush but I'm sure it wasn't anything to be scared about. The boys just need to travel in pairs while we are out here. You never know when you will come across a wild animal or ornery cow." Mike replied.

Maggie called out to Clara, who was still laying in the trailer. "Clara time for breakfast will you grab the plates and utensils when you come out?"

Clara walked out of the trailer carrying the plates. They were now ready for Joey's favorite meal of the day when on a camping trip. They had pancakes, eggs, bacon, & left over dutch oven potatoes. They all sat at the picnic table eating and thinking about what they were going to do for the day while the smell of bacon wafted through the air. Well, except Steve & Joey. In the last two days they had run across some sort of creature that seemed to be spying on them. They weren't sure what it was but in their young minds they had no doubt that it was the same type of creature that had chased the students in the newspaper.

19

Terry pulled into the hospital and relayed to dispatch that he was going to be out of his car at the hospital. He then walked into the hospital to find out what condition Becky was in. As he walked in the front door of the emergency room he heard a message come over the speakers.

"Code Blue trauma one. Code Blue trauma one."

He was hoping this wasn't being called for Becky but deep down he knew otherwise.

He walked up to the front desk where the receptionist asked what she could do for him. He told her whom he was looking for and she told him currently Becky was being attended to in Trauma room one and unfortunately she couldn't give him anymore information. He asked if any family members had been contacted and she stated unfortunately they didn't have any contact information for her. Terry thanked her and told her he was going to see if he could find out how to get a hold of the family.

Terry walked back outside, the sun was starting to warm the valley and he was guessing it was going to be a beautiful day, other than the drama that was unfolding in front of him. He walked over to his patrol car and pulled out his cell phone. He dialed Rob's number but there was no answer. He then tried to call Jake on the off chance that the boys had found his phone and still there was no answer. Terry sighed trying to think about what to do next. A thought came to his mind. He leaned against the hood of the car and dialed Cherryton University's Public Safety office. He was hoping that they could either give him Becky's parent's number or that they would be willing to get into contact with them.

"Cherryton University Public Safety this is Anna."

"Hi Anna this is Terry Johnson with the Cherryton Police Dept. There is a girl by the name of Becky Silverton that goes to the University and she was in an accident last night up the canyon. I was wondering if you could give me her parents phone number so I can let them know what happened?"

"We don't normally give out private student information but let me run it past my Supervisor and make sure it is ok."

"Thanks Anna"

Anna came back to the phone after a few minutes, "Officer Johnson, I have Becky's parents' contact information. Are you ready for it?"

Terry grabbed a pen and paper and wrote down the phone number for Becky's parents.

"Thanks Anna."

Terry hung up the phone and dialed the phone number on the paper. The phone rang three times and then went to voicemail. He left a message on the phone. "Hi this is Officer Johnson with the Cherryton police dept. Please give me a call as soon as you can."

Terry walked back into the hospital and told the receptionist that he had the phone number and had left a message. He also gave the phone number to the receptionist so the hospital would have Becky's parents' phone number. Since there was nothing else he could do here he headed back out the door and towards his patrol car. Terry got in the car and called dispatch letting them know that he was back on duty.

20

Around the time Terry was at the hospital the Jacob's family was finishing up breakfast and about five miles away from them as the crow flies Gabe and the fire department were just finishing cleaning up the damage from the wreck. The tow truck had arrived and loaded Becky's car up. They were picking the pieces of the car that had broken off and then they would open the road to traffic.

Frank, the tow truck driver, called over to Gabe "Hey Gabe, will you come over here? You may want to secure this before I take the car."

Gabe walked over to the car and Frank showed him the gun laying on the floor.

"I wonder why she had this, was she trying to commit suicide?" Frank asked.

"No, she was up here looking for her boyfriend whom she thought may be in danger" Gabe replied. He then proceeded to tell Frank the story about what had happened and why she was worried about Rob & Jake.

"Geez, quite the story, she must have been really concerned to drive up in the middle of the night and to bring a gun along with her."

"Thanks for pointing it out Frank, I will go grab an inventory bag and take her phone and the gun so I can get her items back to her." Gabe went and grabbed a bag used for evidence. He walked back to the car and picked up the gun, he checked if it was loaded and then emptied the clip, there were five rounds missing out of the clip, Gabe was unsure whether the rounds had been fired or if they just hadn't been loaded. He looked under the seat and saw that two shells were laying on the floor.

"What the hell is going on." he thought.

He then picked up Becky's phone and placed it in the bag. He wondered if her parents had been contacted and then his mind went to Rob.

"Was he in real trouble, was Becky involved in their disappearance? Or was he at home in bed and just hadn't called Becky."

Gabe was hoping for the second option. They already had one severely injured person in this story and he was hoping that the worst was over.

After most of the debris had been picked up and loaded onto the tow truck Gabe waved to the driver and he headed down the canyon with the remnants of the car, followed by the fire engine. Gabe was the last vehicle stopped on the road, he jumped into his truck and pulled off the side of the road. He then called out on the radio for the officers that had been directing traffic to start allowing the vehicles through. A few minutes later traffic began flowing.

Gabe pulled into the lane headed up the canyon. He was going to stop and talk to Jim for a moment and then head to where the report had stated Becky, Rob, & Jake had camped the night before. While he assumed that Becky had checked up there already since she was headed down the canyon, he wanted to make sure he had all of the information when he gave Terry an update.

21

After breakfast the Jacobs family cleaned up the dishes. Steve & Joey threw a baseball back and forth while George, Mike, & Charles finished drinking their coffee. Maggie, Clara, Katrina, & Gloria were in their trailers getting ready for the day and Marie was at the picnic table coloring. "Hey dad, can Joey & I take the four wheeler for a ride?"

"Why don't you wait for a little bit, let's figure out what we are doing today and then you can take it out."

Steve sighed and went back to throwing the baseball back and forth with Joey. He would much rather be exploring but after his encounters with the moose or cows or whatever was out there he felt too nervous to go explore.

"What do you want to do today Dad?" George asked.

"I don't know, I figured we could either head up to Aspen Grove Lake where we could fish and let the kids swim around or go for a hike up the canyon. The water is too damned cold for me at the lake but I know those kids won't mind. Either today or tomorrow your mom & I are going to take a ride up the canyon to find wildflowers. What are your thoughts?"

"Maybe we should drive up to Aspen Grove Lake today since it seems like it is going to be a nice day, you never know what type of weather you're going to get from day to day up here. What do you think, Mike?"

"Sounds good to me, I know the kids won't care one way or the other as long as they are having a good time."

"Hey boys, do you want to go up to the lake today and swim around and do some paddle boarding?" George yelled.

"Sounds good to us, Steve said as he ran to catch an errant pass from Joey."

"Alright it is just after nine now we will leave here between 9:30-10 that way we are there before it gets too crowded" Charles said.

"Are you going to go crack the whip on the ladies Dad?" Mike said with a chuckle.

"No way, I'm going to go in the trailer and pack your mom & I a lunch. I would suggest you do the same or it will be you getting something cracked over your head!" Charles said, grinning as he walked away.

George & Mike finished their coffee and headed towards their trailers to let their wives know the plan for the day and to start packing up the towels, coolers, and whatever else they may need at the lake.

"Hey Clara, do you mind making some sandwiches while your mom finishes getting ready and I pack up the towels & cooler?"

"I guess, what are we going to do today anyways?"

"We are going to head up to the lake and you kids can go swimming at the beach or if the water is too cold you can explore the trails and we can maybe do some fishing."

"Did you hear the plan Maggie?"

"Yes I did, it sounds good to me. I will finish getting ready and then I will help you load up the truck. Are the boys being good?"

"Yes they are just outside throwing the baseball around."

"Good, they gave us quite the scare earlier today. I just wanted to make sure they weren't too bothered by their encounter. Moose scare the shit out of me, if the boys were to get stomped on they wouldn't stand a chance."

"I know dear. It was still early enough they may have just startled it as it was trying to get a drink of water from the creek."

22

Gabe pulled up to Jim's patrol truck and rolled his window down.

"Hey Jim, how are you?"

"Doing fine Gabe, did you get the mess cleaned up down there?"

"Yeah she did quite a number on her car, probably would have been better off hitting whatever made her swerve."

"Yeah you never know, maybe it was a car coming the other direction that had made her swerve and she just didn't have time to correct?"

"Yeah that is true I had just assumed it was a deer."

"Very well could have been a deer Gabe, especially since there weren't any other skid marks. I wonder what she was doing up here so early anyways."

"She was up here looking for her boyfriend."

"Awe the jealous type I see," Jim said with a laugh.

"Not quite. Wednesday night Becky, the girl in the accident, her boyfriend Rob and their friend Jake were up here camping and supposedly an animal tried to drag Jake out of camp. He had lost his cellphone so last night Rob & Jake came back up looking for Jake's cell phone. Becky called Terry Johnson with Cherryton Police last night very concerned because the boys hadn't made it back to town. From what it looks like she headed up here looking for them. I'm going to drive up the road and see if I can see their car or any clues."

"Do you want some backup?"

"Yeah that may be good, I'm not sure what I'm going to find when I get up there."

"Alright you lead the way Gabe."

Gabe turned around and drove up the road with Jim behind him. They continued driving up to the lake turn around but Gabe didn't see what he was looking for. Gabe stopped and Jim pulled up next to him. "Did you see them anywhere Gabe?"

"No, they are driving a green Subaru and I had assumed they were up here in the paved campground but I didn't see them. They are either camped off the North Fork road or they aren't up here. I'm going to drive up the North Fork road a little way and see if I can spot their car, do you have time to follow me?"

"Yeah, let me radio in to dispatch while we are up here and I will let them know we are going to check the road out."

"Good idea Terry should hear the radio traffic as well and will know we are still looking into this, I'm sure he is at the hospital attempting to talk to Becky."

They drove the two miles back to the North Fork road of Aspen Grove and made a left hand turn to head up the road. They were only up the road about a mile before they found what they had been looking for. There was Rob's green Subaru, the passenger door ajar. Gabe immediately had the hair on the back of his neck stand up, he knew something seemed off even if nothing looked out of the ordinary just yet.

He pulled up right behind Rob's car and looked around. It didn't look like anybody was around, but why would Rob leave his door open? Jim pulled up next to Gabe and looked over at him and asked "is this the car?"

Gabe nodded yes. Both of them climbed out of their trucks and walked to the back of the Subaru.

"I'm going to go have a peek inside since the door is open and see if I can see anything out of the ordinary."

Gabe walked up to the driver's side door and looked in. Nothing seemed wrong, there wasn't any blood or any signs of forced entry.

"ROB, JAKE" Gabe yelled. No answer.

"Maybe they wandered over into the tree looking for Jake's phone." Jim said.

"It's possible but something just doesn't seem right."

"Gut feeling?"

"Yeah something just felt wrong as soon as we pulled up, I don't know what it is."

"Well Gabe if there is one thing I have learned working in this field it is to trust my gut, so if yours is saying something is wrong maybe we should do a little more investigating."

"Ok, let's secure our vehicles and have a look around."

They both walked over to the fire ring to see if they noticed anything. They could see boot prints and what looked like an animal track but it had been disturbed so they couldn't tell what the animal tracks were.

"Everything looks normal. I don't see anything too concerning." Jim said.

They then walked over to the group of pines that were on the other side of the camp. From what Gabe had read in the police report that Terry had sent him, this must be where the animal had tried to drag Jake two nights ago. As they got over toward the tree Jim thought he heard something move in the brush alongside the pines. He grabbed Gabe's shoulder and they both stopped. "Did you hear that?" Jim asked.

"No, what was it?"

"I'm not sure I thought I heard something move over in the brush."

"ROB. JAKE. ARE YOU HERE? I NEED TO TALK TO YOU BECKY HAS BEEN IN A BAD ACCIDENT."

Still they didn't hear a response. They were looking over toward the brush and saw movement heading away from them.

"Hey stop right there!" Jim yelled.

Whatever was moving didn't stop so they assumed it may be a cow or deer that they may have scared away. They started making their way towards the pines again. As they walked into the opening both of their eyes got big. There were animal tracks everywhere, although these looked more like human tracks with claws rather than animal tracks.

"HOLY SHIT! Look at those tracks! They are huge!" Jim said.

"Yeah they are what the hell are they." Gabe asked.

"I don't know, you're the animal expert. If you were to ask me it looks like bigfoot has been in here."

Gabe rolled his eyes at Jim.

"Sorry Gabe the smartass in me just can't stay contained for too long. I don't know what these tracks are. It almost looks like someone was walking on the balls of their feet and haven't cut their toenails in a year."

"Jim, will you go grab some evidence tape and we will tape the area off. I know we don't know if a crime has been committed but I don't want this area disturbed I would like to know what has been walking around here."

Jim headed off back towards the trucks and Gabe bent down and took a few pictures. He was just finishing up as Jim brought the tape back.

"Let's get this roped off and then we can keep looking for evidence."

Jim headed left with the tape and Gabe went right. As Jim was walking toward the far end of the pines he looked down and thought he saw a few drops of dried blood. He looked down through the brush and saw what looked to him like something had been dragged through the brush.

"Hey Gabe, you may want to come and look at this," he yelled. Gabe finished taping off his side of the pines and headed towards Jim.

"What is it Jim?"

"Look here at the ground, those look like drag marks and that looks like dried blood."

"Yeah it does, come on let's see where they go.

Gabe & Jim slowly started following the drag marks through the brush. The marks were easy to follow at first because the branches had been broken but as they entered a field full of prairie grass and sage brush it started getting a little harder. Every 150 feet or so they would leave a marker so if they lost the trail they would have somewhere to restart. They continued tracking through sage brush, willows, and wildflower patches. By the time they had tracked the trail for close to half a mile the tracks seemed to just disappear.

"Alright Gabe, I think we are going to need to get a bigger search party out here. We can go back to our last spot and try to find the trail again but I think this would go quicker if we had more help."

"Yeah, you're right. Why don't you go back up to the lake and make a call to dispatch letting them know what is going on and requesting search and rescue as well as more officers. While you do that I'm going to continue to see if I can find the tracks and follow them."

"Alright, make sure you keep placing markers down so when I get

back up here I can find you."

Jim turned around and started back tracking their trail to the trucks and Gabe went back to the last marker and started searching for the tracks again.

It took Jim roughly fifteen minutes to find his way back to the trucks. As he walked around the grove of pine trees he saw something move off to his right. He couldn't tell what it was because it moved quickly into the brush and off into the trees. He waited and watched for a few minutes but didn't see anything else so he continued to work his way around the pines watching along the ground for any evidence that he may see. The tracks were still perplexing to him. He was a hunter and considered himself a fairly good tracker, yet these were tracks he had never seen before.

As Jim walked up to his truck he immediately noticed a few tracks along the side of the truck and there was some black fur that looked like it may belong to a bear on the ground. "Maybe there is an old sick bear wandering around, but the tracks just don't match the animal," he thought to himself. Jim climbed into his truck and pulled away. He knew the closest spot he would be able to get a signal was up by the lake so that is where he would head.

23

Terry was driving down main street when his phone began to ring. He pulled into a Wal-Mart parking lot and looked down at his phone. It was the hospital calling him.

"Hello, this is Officer Johnson."

"Hi Terry this is Suzette from the hospital, I just wanted to let you know I was able to get a hold of Becky's parents and they will be here in about two hours."

"That's great how is Becky doing"

"Well I can't give a whole lot of information but she is currently being moved to the ICU."

"Ok thank you Suzette, will you please let me know when her parents have arrived I would like to come talk to them."

"Sure thing, I will give you a call when they arrive."

After Terry hung up he felt some relief that at least Becky's parents had heard what had happened and would be on their way to see her.

While he was sitting there he wondered what was taking Gabe so long to get back to him. He should have had the wreck cleaned up by now and made it to Bear Lake. He looked out his passenger window at the Starbucks that was across the parking lot and decided to go get a coffee. He walked in and ordered himself a Grande Mocha Latte and waited for it to be made. Just as his name was called to let him know his drink had been made his phone began to ring again, this time it was his wife Joselyn.

"Hi honey can you give me just a minute?"

He turned to the Barista and said thank you and grabbed his cup of coffee. He then went and sat down at a table so he could talk on the phone.

"I'm back, sorry about that I was just ordering a coffee, is everything alright?

"Geez, it must be a busy day if you are having more coffee. Yes everything is fine, I just wanted to see how your day was going and see if that girl Becky was ok."

"It's going ok, I still haven't heard back from Gabe so I don't know what is going on up the canyon. I spent most of the morning at the hospital. I was trying to track Becky's parents down so they would know what is going on."

"Did you get a hold of them"

"Well kind of, I had to call the University to get her phone number and when I called them they didn't answer. The hospital was able to get a hold of them though and they are on their way down."

"That's good news, how is she doing?"

"The hospital told me she is in the ICU, but wouldn't give me any other updates. I'm hoping to speak to her parents once they arrive."

"Well I will let you get back to work. Let me know if you are going to be home late or on time so I can plan on picking up dinner on my way home or if we are going to go out."

"Ok, I will, I love you."

Terry hung up the phone and headed outside again. He immediately regretted not getting an iced coffee as he could tell it was going to get warm today. Terry got back in his car and decided to head into the office to read back through the kids police report and see if he could see any details that he may have missed.

24

"Alright everyone let's head out." George yelled.

Joey threw Steve one last pass and ran over to Mike's truck to get in. Steve ran over to the trailer and yelled "Mom & Clara let's go!"

"We are coming. Steve, give Clara and I just a minute to put everything away."

Steve walked over to the truck.

"Mom said her and Clara needed to put away their makeup and then they would be out."

"Ok thanks Steve, why don't you go over and tell your Grandma & Grandpa that we are leaving."

Steve got to Charles and Gloria's trailer just as Gloria was coming out.

"Grandma, are you ready to go?"

"I sure am Steve, will you teach me to paddle board?"

"Of course but the water might be a little cold."

"Oh, well I guess I better sit this one out," she said.

Charles was right behind Gloria and Steve asked him if he would come paddle boarding with him.

"Well Steve I would but I have a hole in the knee of my swimsuit so I will just have to sit and watch you this time. Tell your dad that we will follow you up to the lake."

"Ok Grandpa see you there."

Steve walked back over to his dad's truck and told him that Charles & Gloria would follow them out of the campground. He looked over at Mike's trailer he could see his uncle locking up the trailer as his family was climbing into his truck. He waved over at Joey and Joey waved back.

"See you at the lake, Joey."

Steve was starting to get impatient with his mom and sister. He was ready to leave and they were always waiting on those two. Just as he was about to yell at them to hurry up they both came out of the trailer. Clara & Steve both climbed into the truck as Maggie was locking up the trailer.

"Alright let's go to the lake" Steve yelled out in excitement.

George started up his truck and they headed down the bumpy road. As they headed down the road they passed the camp that had been torn apart by the cows. It looked as though no one had been to the camp yet because it looked like it was still in disarray.

"Steve, I've been thinking of this morning and what was between you and Joey the more I'm thinking it was probably a cow," George said.

"Yeah it probably was, it was just big and scared us."

"Well cows can be just as dangerous as any other animal so it is better to be safe than sorry, especially if it was an ornery bull."

"We will stay together from now on so at least there will be two of us to try and scare off anything that comes around."

"It's also good to make noise as you're walking so that you don't startle an animal by accidentally sneaking up on it."

"I know dad, you told us that last year when we were up here."

"STEVE, it was just a reminder, don't be cranky with your Dad."

"Ok mom, sorry Dad."

George looked back at Steve and smiled. He was a good kid but the apple sure didn't fall from the tree, he remembered getting annoyed with his dad when Charles would remind him to be careful when he was younger as well.

The rest of the ride was uneventful. All three trucks pulled onto the highway and headed down towards the turn off for Aspen Grove. As they headed up the road a Sheriff's truck came to a stop on one of the dirt roads and waited for them to pass. George let off the gas to slow down a little bit.

"Sneaky spot to be watching for speeders,."

Maggie looked over at him, "Luckily your dad is following us or we would be on the side of the road right now."

"I probably wouldn't have been speeding."

Maggie rolled her eyes her husband usually was speeding even when he wasn't running late.

As they pulled into the parking lot at Aspen Lake the Sheriff's truck was still behind them and George started thinking that he might be getting a ticket after all. George parked his truck, Mike & Charles followed suit. As they did, the Sheriff's truck passed by and pulled into a parking spot further from the lake.

Jim pulled into a parking spot where he thought he knew he could get a strong radio signal. He then called down to dispatch and requested that Sheriff Alan Hamilton radio him back on a different channel. He didn't want word getting out that there was a possible serious situation up the canyon when the drag marks may be something not tied to the boys and they could have been out hiking.

A few minutes later the Sheriff called him on the channel he had requested and he told the Sheriff what had happened. The Sheriff was concerned about sending a large search party out when there wasn't even a report of anyone missing. The Sheriff agreed to send two more deputy's and would request six team members of the Search and Rescue. Jim thanked him and put his radio down. He then decided he would go and talk to the people that had just pulled up and see if they had seen anything out of the ordinary and if they would keep an eye out for the boys.

George and his family had unloaded most everything from the trucks, there was only a cooler left. While the rest of the family started setting up their picnic spot for the day George and Mike headed back to the truck to grab the cooler. As they approached the truck the Sheriff's deputy that had followed them into the parking lot stopped next to them and got out of his truck.

"Howdy Officer, how are you doing today?"

"Well it's been a pretty busy day so far, a few miles down the road very early this morning there was a one vehicle crash and now we are looking for two boys that may be missing."

"Wow, that does seem like a busy day. How old are the boys that you are looking for?"

"Well I guess they aren't boys they are college students so they are in their early 20's."

"Oh ok, where did they go missing from?"

"The boys we are looking for are friends with the person that was injured in the wreck this morning so we mainly want to talk to them about that and see if they have any information that may help us. Are you guys up here for just the day?"

"Yeah we are up here at the lake for just the day but we are camped up Fredericks Basin for the weekend."

"That's a nice place to be, I hope you have a good time. If you guys see two that may match the following description will you please ask them if their names are Rob & Jake please let them know that we are looking for them."

Jim then gave them a description of Rob & Jake.

"Of course Officer."

"Thanks."

Jim turned around and started towards his truck. He then paused and turned around.

"You guys haven't noticed anything strange while you were camped up Fredericks Basin have you?"

"Well we only got up there yesterday, but other than cows being all over the place and knocking a few things over I haven't noticed anything strange," George replied.

"What did they knock over?"

George then told the officer about the campsite that had been ravaged.

"Wow, that is something else. Hopefully the people will learn their lesson to leave their stuff out when they leave."

"Hey officer, what is going on up in Chapel Fork?" Mike asked.

"What do you mean?"

"Well we all read in the newspaper how some kids had been attacked at a campsite and I was just curious if you had any information or if you had figured out what had chased them."

"Well we had another development yesterday, this complaint actually came from up here in the North Fork of Aspen Grove. We had three college kids that claimed one was almost dragged out of his campsite Wednesday night."

Jim didn't want to tell them it was the same kids that were now missing. He was still having a hard time believing the story and thought that the kids maybe had a little too much to drink or had taken some other drug that made them hallucinate and see things that weren't actually happening. He figured until there was more evidence there was no reason to cause paranoia in people trying to enjoy their weekend.

George looked shocked, "I hadn't heard about that, do you think there is any reason to be concerned?"

"You should keep an eye out on your kids but with the little evidence that we currently have I don't see any reason that you shouldn't enjoy your weekend."

"Ok officer, well thanks for the information, we will keep an eye out for the two guys and if we see them we will tell them that you were wanting to talk to them. Do you by chance have a business card we can give them?"

"Oh yes I do, here you go. Go enjoy the day with your family. It looks like it is going to be beautiful!"

Jim climbed back in his truck and headed back to where Gabe was parked. He wanted to make sure that Gabe knew what assistance they were getting.

George & Mike grabbed the cooler and headed back to join their families at the beach. "Hey Mike, do you think we should be concerned at all with what is going on?"

"We should probably keep an eye on the kids just to make sure that if there is a wild bear that has rabies or something they aren't attacked but the chances that there would be a bear attacking people up in Chapel Fork as well as here is very unlikely. My guess is the people that reported the story up here had already seen the story up Chapel Fork and wanted to get in on the story."

"Yeah you're probably right. I guess between the story we heard from Jim and the camp that is destroyed up Fredericks Basin I may be acting a little paranoid."

"I'm sure everything is fine George. We probably should keep the details of the interaction from the family though or I think our trip will be cut short."

"Yeah I agree, what they don't know won't hurt them."

George was looking out on the lake, there were at least ten fishing boats already out there and George assumed it was only going to get busier.

As they got down to the beach Maggie walked up to George & Mike and asked what the Sheriff's deputy had wanted. They told her about the crash and that the Sheriff's Dept. was looking for the boys to let them know about the accident as well as ask them about any details that they may have.

"Well I hope the person in the wreck was alright."

"He didn't tell us much about it, of course we didn't ask about it either," George responded.

They sat the cooler down and Steve ran up to his dad.

"Hey dad can we pump up the paddleboards?"

"It's still a little cold don't you think?"

"It will be warm by the time we get the paddleboards pumped up."

"Alright go start getting them out of their bags and I will be right over."

George grabbed Mike & himself a Coke out of the cooler and they headed over to help the boys pump up the paddleboards.

Maggie, Katrina, Gloria, & Clara sat in their chairs soaking up the sun as Marie looked for rocks along the shore.

Charles picked up his fishing equipment and said, "Well I'm going to head down the shoreline a little ways and see if I can't catch us some dinner."

Gloria looked at him and smiled. "Be careful dear, I don't want the boys to have to come drag you out of the lake."

"I will be fine. I may be old but I still have my balance."

Charles headed down the beach and around a bend in the shoreline. It was looking like it was going to be a fabulous day on the lake.

25

Terry walked into the Police station and over to his desk. He sat down and turned on his computer. He was going to do his due diligence and read the police report from Rob, Jake, & Becky one more time. As he pulled up the document on his computer his phone rang. It was Sheriff Hamilton calling to talk to him.

"Officer Johnson?"

"This is him, how are you Sheriff?"

"I'm doing well. I'm calling you about a situation up the canyon."

Sheriff Hamilton continued by telling Terry about what was going on and the request made by Jim.

"Would you be able to send me over the police report that you wrote up yesterday? We need to get to the bottom of this and I think it would help if the Sheriff's Dept and Police Dept. worked together on this."

"That's not a problem sir I will send it over to you right now, but you should know Fish & Game currently is the leading department on this case. We sent it over to them yesterday since it has to do with an animal problem up the canyon."

"As you know Terry they are short staffed so I'm sure they would appreciate the help. I'm not trying to step on anyone's toes or get into a pissing match, I just want to make sure our Deputies and Search and Rescue members know exactly what is going on."

"I agree with you Sheriff, I will send this over right now. I'm going to head over to the hospital in a little bit and speak with Becky's family. I will call and give your department a rundown of what I find out."

"Thanks Terry, I appreciate it."

Terry hung up the phone and read through the police report one more time. He didn't see anything that stood out to him. He printed out the report and walked over to the fax machine and faxed the document over to the Sheriff's office.

Terry walked back over to his desk and shut his computer down. He then headed back out to his car and let dispatch know he was back on duty. He was asked to go watch for people speeding heading past the college and up the canyon. Friday's were one of the busier travel days up the canyon and people were always in a rush to get to their vacation spot. He figured he would be able to patrol the road for an hour before he headed back to the hospital. He was hoping by then Becky's parents would be at the hospital and he would be able to speak with them.

26

Jim drove back to the north fork road and parked next to Gabe's truck. He tried to radio Gabe to let him know that there was help on the way and that maybe he should head back to the trucks to wait for help. Unfortunately he couldn't figure out what channel Gabe's radio was on.

"We should have chosen a radio channel before we separated, what an amateur move," he thought to himself.

He knew it would be roughly two hours before help would arrive so he decided to write a note and leave it on his window so the Deputies & Search and Rescue teams would see it and know where they were at.

Jim tucked the note under his windshield wiper and headed down the trail to go find Gabe. He walked past the pine tree grove and was careful to keep an eye out for anything that moved. This seemed to be a hotspot for attacks based on the drag marks they were following as well the story Gabe had told him about Jake being attacked. He slowly made his way back to the drag mark and then began following the markers that they had left to make the trail easier to find. It would take him roughly fifteen minutes to get to the spot he had left Gabe and then he would have to follow Gabe's trail to wherever he had progressed.

As Jim got down to the spot he had left Gabe he noticed there were no more markers marking the trail. Jim knew Gabe had plenty of flags to mark the trail so he wasn't sure which way to go. "GABE" he yelled, hoping that Gabe was still searching for the lost trail and wouldn't be too far away. Jim yelled one more time and then heard rustling from further down the canyon. He slowly started walking that way. He was ready to pull his gun if needed but didn't want to pull it out on another officer. Gabe came walking out of a patch of willows and aspens, he was down where the creek would be running this time of year. Gabe waved his hand for Jim to come down to him. Jim walked through the sage brush and grass down to where Gabe was standing.

"Were you able to get us any help?"

"Yeah I talked to the Sheriff and he is sending up a couple of team members from the Search and Rescue as well as a couple of Deputies to help us with the search. Did you make any more progress on the trail we were following?"

"Well I can't seem to find any sign of the trail after we lost it back there but come look down here in the river, there is something interesting I need to show you."

Jim followed Gabe down to the creek bed and he could see the footprints from the attacker he could also see what looked like heel marks from shoes being dragged into the water. "Do you see those?" Gabe asked.

"Yeah I can see them, it just doesn't make sense. If Rob or Jake were attacked and dragged down the mountainside we would have seen the drag marks continue on."

"Unless whatever it was picked him up and carried them from that spot to here."

Jim looked perplexed and then stated "I don't know how any animal would be able to pick up a grown man and carry him 200 yards in steep rough terrain."

"And what type of animal would know to cover their tracks by carrying them through the water?" Gabe asked.

"The only one I can think of would be a human, but there is no way a human would be able to carry a grown man through this terrain."

"I know, but what if there is some other creature that we have never encountered?"

"Good hell Gabe are you trying to say that Bigfoot is real and is up here attacking people?"

"I'm not stating anything other than we need to make sure we keep our mind open to what may be happening. None of this makes sense so we need to make sure we don't send out searchers without them having knowledge of exactly what we have found so far."

Jim shook his head, "Yeah you are right, we don't want to send out searchers into harm's way without them knowing the full extent. Whatever is going on out here we need to get to the bottom of it."

Gabe & Jim took pictures and marked the spot of the drag marks into the creek. They then headed back up the mountain to wait for their backup to arrive. Gabe wanted to get back to his truck anyway, it was almost 11:30 and he hadn't eaten anything since breakfast.

27

Up at Aspen lake the Jacobs family was enjoying the warmth of the sun. Steve, Joey , & Marie were playing in the water.

"Hey kids, why don't you come have a snack?" Maggie called.

"We don't want one right now mom we aren't hungry," stated Steve.

"Come have a snack you guys need to have a break from the water, it is freezing."

The kids slowly started walking out of the water and up the beach. All three of them had blue lips and were shivering from being so cold.

"See I told you guys that you needed a break, your lips are blue!"

"Aunt Maggie, we weren't cold until we got out of the water," Joey said.

Maggie smiled and giggled to herself. She knew that Joey's story wasn't true but she didn't want to argue with him.

"Ok well let's get some food in you and then you can go back to the water and swim if you like. I have some chocolate chip zucchini bread for you to munch on as well as a bottle of chocolate milk. Does that sound good?"

"YUM" said Marie through her chattering teeth.

Maggie sliced them each a piece of bread and had Clara pour them glasses of chocolate milk. They all sat down on their towels and ate their snacks in silence.

"Well I'm going to go check on Dad. Do you want to come with me, Clara?" George asked.

"No thanks."

"Come on, you have been a bump on a log since we got here. Let's go check on Grandpa."

Maggie chimed in "Clara, go for a walk with your dad. He is scared to go alone and needs someone to watch over him so he doesn't get lost."

Everyone laughed at Maggie's comment including George.

"Fine, let's go Dad."

Clara got up from her chair and grabbed a Coke out of the cooler.

"Hey will you grab me one also Clara?" George asked.

Clara reached back into the cooler and grabbed another Coke. She then walked over and handed it to George.

"We will be back in a few minutes, Dad was just going to go around this bend."

George and Clara started down the trail, it was a beautiful view with the sun reflecting off of the crystal clear water and the snow-capped mountain peaks behind. As they walked they were looking for fish in the water. They could see the bottom of the lake for as far out as they could see. This made the bottom of the lake look like it was shallow but in reality it was just so clear that you could see fifteen feet down to the bottom.

They walked the two hundred or so yards to where the shoreline curved and the lake widened. They were expecting to see Charles here but he was nowhere in sight.

"Isn't this where Grandpa was supposed to be Dad?"

"Yes but you know your Grandpa he probably kept wandering down the shore if he didn't get a bite."

"How far do you think he went?"

"I'm not sure we will just have to follow the shoreline, I doubt he went much further."

They continued to walk the shoreline looking for Charles. George led the way, he wanted to shield his daughter in case Charles had fallen into the lake or something horrible had happened. After hiking down the shoreline for another ten minutes they were able to hear Charles talking to someone.

George turned back to Clara. "Well I guess he went further than I thought!"

"Ya think! I'm glad I brought a drink because if we are going to wait for Grandpa to finish talking we may be here a while."

George laughed. "Yeah you know how your Grandpa loves to tell fishing stories to people, especially strangers!"

As they walked through some brush they could see Charles down by the water talking to a man. The man looked pretty scraggly but George didn't think much of it since when people were camping they tended to look dirtier than normal.

"Hey Dad there you are."

"Uh-oh I'm going to be in trouble for wandering," Charles said while grinning.

"You found me!"

"Yeah we could hear you from down the trail telling one of your fishing stories Grandpa."

"Yeah but this story is true. George I was telling Harry about the eight pound trout you caught in this lake when you were fifteen."

"Yeah it was a big fish and that story is actually true," said George.

"Hi Harry, I'm George, Charles' son. This is Clara, my daughter. Are you up here camping?"

"Yeah my family and I are tent camping up here for a few more days."

"Sounds like fun, are you doing any fishing?"

"Yeah a little bit. We caught a couple last night and ate them for dinner. I was just coming down to take a dip in the lake when I came across Charles fishing."

"Well I better get back to my camp so my wife & kids aren't wondering where I'm at. Nice to meet you guys."

"You to Harry, maybe we will see you around." George replied.

The three of them waved to Harry as he headed down the trail.

"He seemed kind of odd and standoffish if you ask me," George said.

Clara also chimed in, "Yeah that dude seemed a little off."

"You two are paranoid, he was perfectly fine until you two showed up. We had been talking for about fifteen minutes. He told me about a couple of hikes he had been on and how he was enjoying his time up here."

"Have you caught any fish yet Dad?"

"I had a few bites a while ago but nothing since, that's why I moved down here, but I'm not having much luck here either."

"How much longer do you plan on fishing?" George asked.

"I don't know, I think I will cast a line in and sit for about ten minutes and then head back."

"Alright Clara & I will wait for you."

They all sat down on the side of the lake and enjoyed the warmth & beauty of the day.

28

Terry had been patrolling the canyon road around the University for about two hours when he decided to head back to the hospital. He was hoping to talk to Becky's parents about Becky's relationship with Rob and see if anything had seemed strange. He primarily wanted to know if the three were using drugs or not as this could weigh heavily into the cause of the accident as well as into their story about the camping trip.

As Terry pulled into the hospital parking lot dispatch called him on his cell phone.

"Hi Terry, it's Lisa. I was asked by the Sheriff to give you an update on the search going on up the canyon."

"Great! Have they found the boys yet?"

"No, they are still searching. Deputy Jim Griffin called and requested some more people to head up the canyon. They are going to send a few Deputies as well as the Search & Rescue."

"Wow, have they found any sign of them?"

"Well there were some drag marks that they are trying to track but we aren't even sure if that is from the boys. There were also some strange animal prints that the Sheriff was told about so they are trying to figure out what type of animal left them."

"Ok, well will you let the Sheriff know that if they are still searching I'm going to head up the canyon to help after my shift. I will be off around five."

"Sure thing Terry, we will keep you updated."

"Thanks Lisa."

Terry hung up the phone, walked into the hospital and headed over to the receptionist.

"Hi Suzette, how are you?"

"I'm doing well Terry. I assume you are here to see Becky's parents?"

"Yes, are they here?"

"They are in Becky's room getting updated by the Dr. I will text the nurse that is working and ask that she let me know when the Dr. has left."

"Ok, no rush. I'm going to go sit outside for a little bit. Would you mind coming and getting me when they are ready?"

"Yes, no problem at all."

"Thank you."

Terry headed back outside with his coffee and sat down on a bench under a tree. He sat there for a while watching traffic go by. After about twenty minutes he saw Suzette come out of the hospital and waive him over.

"Terry the Dr. is out of the room and Becky's dad is going to meet you in an office that is just outside the ICU. You will be meeting him on the second floor, room 218."

"Thanks Suzette."

Terry headed over to the elevator and pressed the button to go up. He walked out of the elevator and took a right heading down the hallway towards the ICU. Right before he would have entered the ICU he saw room 218 on his left. He opened the door expecting to see someone but nobody was there. He sat down and waited for Becky's dad to arrive.

A few minutes later the door opened and a man walked in followed by the nurse.

"Here you are Mr. Silverton," the nurse said. She then turned around and walked back towards the ICU.

Terry stood up and reached out his hand towards the man.

"Hi I'm officer Terry Johnson."

The man took Terry's hand.

"Nice to meet you, I'm Trevor Silverton. I understand you wanted to talk to me about my daughter?"

"Yes Mr. Silverton I did."

"Please call me Trevor."

"First off, if you don't mind me asking how is your daughter doing Trevor?"

"She is in rough shape. From what the Doctor tells us she is lucky to be alive. Becky had a brain bleed plus multiple other injuries including a punctured lung and broken ribs. The Doctor said the next few days will be touch and go, but she expects her to pull through. Is she in some sort of trouble?"

"Not from what I can tell. I was more or less wanting to know about her demeanor the last few weeks. The reason I ask is because of a police report she submitted yesterday."

Terry gave a copy of the police report to Trevor and gave him a minute to read over it. He then proceeded to tell him about the calls he received from Becky last night and what had happened.

"Wow that is quite the story. That is a lot of information to process so quickly."

"I understand if you need a minute Trevor, this is a lot of information."

"No no I'm ok."

"Becky's demeanor hasn't been different lately. She seemed happy when I talked to her last weekend."

"And she didn't use drugs or anything like that?"

"I mean she would have a few drinks like any college kid, but no I didn't know of her to be using any drugs and there hadn't been any signs from what I could tell."

"Has your wife expressed any concerns?"

"No, Diana hasn't mentioned anything to me. I wished she wouldn't have headed up the canyon to find Rob and Jake. I'm sure they are fine. Did you talk to them yet?"

"No we haven't, we are trying to get into contact with them but have had no luck. How is your daughter's relationship with Rob?"

"It seems fine. She hasn't made any comments about the relationship being on the rocks or anything like that?"

"I was just wondering if there was anything that could have caused her to drive erratically and wreck."

"There is nothing Officer, did you ever think it was just an accident?"

"Oh, absolutely. Look, more than likely at the time of night that Becky was driving and an animal ran across the road in front of her. I'm not accusing her of doing anything wrong, I'm just trying to get all of the details so I can share it with the Sheriff's Dept."

"Ok, I'm sorry I didn't mean to snap at you. I'm just very upset right now. My daughter may have brain damage and then the questions from you are just too much. I have never witnessed or seen anything that would make me think my daughter is doing drugs. I don't know if she saw something that upset her up the canyon or not. I'm sorry I don't have anything else to offer."

"One last question. Did your daughter own a gun?"

"No, not that I'm aware of. I know she would go shooting with Rob every once in a while but she didn't own one herself. Why?"

"The deputies that found her after the wreck said there was a pistol and two empty casings on the floor."

"I don't think it would have been hers, but maybe Rob had left it in the car."

"Thank you for your time Trevor. We will keep in touch and I hope Becky heals quickly."

"Please let me know when you have found Rob."

"I will keep you updated. I'm sure the boys just decided to stay the night and are out hiking somewhere. We will talk to you later."

Terry opened the office door and let Trevor leave first. He watched as Trevor entered the ICU doors and he truly hoped Becky would be ok.

29

As Gabe & Jim walked around the pines and came into view of their trucks Gabe saw he had a flat tire.

"Son of a bitch, how did I get a flat tire?"

"I saw it when I came up earlier and I forgot to tell you. I'm wondering if you ran over something down by the accident site."

"We cleaned it up pretty well, I don't think I would have hit anything." Gabe walked over to his tire and looked at it. He didn't notice any damage to the tire wall so he started inspecting the tire. He slowly started at the rear and worked his way up to the front of it. He couldn't see any damage or anything stuck in the tire.

"I guess I better get my spare out while we wait for the reinforcements to arrive."

Gabe & Jim walked around the back of Gabe's truck and opened his tailgate. Gabe grabbed his jack and handed it to Jim and then he grabbed the rod to lower his spare tire out from underneath the truck bed. He then rolled the tire over to the passenger side of the truck while Jim was raising the jack. Once the tire was almost off of the ground Gabe grabbed his lug wrench and loosened the lug nuts. Jim then finished raising the truck so that the tire was off of the ground. Gabe took the tire off and sat it on the ground. He wanted to inspect it after they finished putting the new tire on.

Jim grabbed the new tire and they both lifted it so it was sitting on the bolts. Jim held the tire in place and Gabe put the lug nuts back on. Once the tire was on Jim lowered the jack and Gabe then tightened the lug nuts.

"Thanks for your help Jim."

"No problem at all."

Jim picked up the jack and placed it in the back of the truck while Gabe rolled the flat tire to the back of the truck. He then lifted it on to the tailgate and began inspecting it to see if he could see where the damage had come from.

After searching for a few minutes and having no luck Gabe decided it was time for lunch. He walked over to the passenger door and reached in to grab his lunchbox.

"You want something Jim? I have an extra sandwich in here if you would like. It looks like it's going to be a long day."

"No thanks, I have a lunch packed as well, I will go grab it."

Gabe placed his lunch box on the seat and pulled out an apple and a ham sandwich. He then sat the lunchbox back on the floor and went back to the tailgate of his truck. He was looking at the tire over again by the time Jim got back.

"Any luck finding the puncture hole Gabe?"

"No, I haven't seen anything yet. It looks like I will just have to take it down to town and have them figure out what I ran over."

"We should have some help up here soon I would think and then we can get this search over with and you can head to town.

30

Rob slowly woke up and opened his eyes, everything was pitch black, he raised his hand but couldn't see it.

He thought to himself "where the hell am I? Am I blind?"

He tried to sit up but that sent his head spinning so he laid back down. He felt the ground and noticed that the floor was dirt. He was trying to remember what happened but all he could remember was he & Jake were looking for Jake's phone and then Jake was gone. He remembered walking back to grab his gun out of the car and that was it. He had no recollection of what had happened to him or how he had been moved.

"What the hell happened to me?" he thought.

Then he started thinking about Jake. "Was he ok? Was he nearby in this same dwelling?"

He wanted to yell out for Jake but didn't want to alert his kidnappers so he decided to keep silent for now.

He slowly sat up again and his head began spinning. He held himself up on his elbows for a few minutes and the pain began to subside. He then started belly crawling hoping to come into contact with a wall so he could try and lift himself up. After crawling a few feet he reached out with his hand and felt a wall. He crawled closer to it and started to rub his hand up and down on the wall.

When he realized that the wall was made of stone he started to get very nervous.

"Am I in a cave? Who brought me here? Was it the same creature that attacked Jake the night before?"

He decided to sit here along the wall for a minute and try to let the pain in his head subside. He reached down to do a self assessment. He felt his legs, arms and body. He didn't feel too much pain other than what felt like some scratches along the back of his shoulders. He then put his hands to his head. He didn't notice any cuts along his face but when he felt the back of his head he realized that the hair had been torn off and he had what felt like road rash on the back of his head. "Was I dragged across the ground?" he thought.

Maybe this was a bear that had attacked him & Jake. But it wouldn't have brought him back to a cave. A bear would have just attacked him and either left or ate him on site, he thought.

He sat there and tried to figure out exactly what had happened but he just couldn't recollect what had happened after he grabbed his gun.

This has to be a large creature he thought to himself.
There is no way a bear would have put me in a cave.
Then he thought, *Is there really a bigfoot?*

He had heard stories over the years about people seeing what they thought was bigfoot up here in the canyon. There was even a show that had interviewed a snow plow driver that had sworn he had seen bigfoot near the Fredericks Basin turnoff. Of course nobody ever had solid proof so everyone thought the stories were always made up.

Now I'm going crazy. There is no such thing as bigfoot or someone would have seen one by now.

Rob then heard something to his left.

"That must be the way to the opening," he said to himself.

Rob lowered back on to his stomach and started crawling in that direction. He kept the wall next to him so he would have some semblance of where he was. He crawled and crawled. After what seemed like forever he reached over to feel the wall and noticed that there seemed to be a corner just ahead. He crawled a little further and confirmed that there was either another section in this tunnel or it turned directly to his left. He leaned back against the wall again and contemplated what to do. He could either turn and follow the wall or try to continue straight and see if there was a wall on the other side. He had two directions that he could go and wasn't sure what to do.

As Rob sat there he thought he felt a breeze coming around the corner of the cave.

Am I really feeling that?

Maybe I'm just imagining it.

At this point he was very tired and thirsty and had no idea when the last time he had drank or ate anything was. He didn't even know how long he had been in the cave. He laid down on the ground for a minute and soon was asleep.

31

"Well I guess I'm not going to have any luck catching fish today. Let's head back to camp. Clara looks bored!" Charles said.

"You said we were only going to stay for another ten minutes Grandpa. It's almost been an hour."

"I know Clara I'm sorry, but at least you had great company!" Charles said.

George laughed and Clara rolled her eyes. They helped Charles get his tacklebox in order while he folded up his fishing pole. They then turned back to the trail and started the walk back to the beach. When they arrived back at the beach Steve, Joey, & Marie were playing in the water while Maggie, Katrina, & Gloria were sitting on the beach watching them.

Maggie looked over at them, "It's about time you guys get back, we were starting to get worried!"

"Sorry Maggie, I kept them waiting while I was fishing." Charles said.

"It's ok Charles I'm sure it was a good time."

"We had a nice time, but Dad was further down the beach than we expected and of course he made a new friend so there wasn't a lot of fishing going on when we found him."

"Leave it to your dad to talk any strangers ear off," Gloria said with a laugh.

"Alright it's time for lunch. Maggie, do you want to help me make sandwiches?" Katrina asked.

"Sure I can help you with that, I think the rest of the food is in the truck."

"Is everyone ok with a turkey sandwich? We will bring the chips back down with us."

Everyone was ok with a turkey sandwich except Joey. He wanted a Peanut Butter and Jelly.

"Leave it to my son to be the difficult kid." Katrina said.

Maggie & Katrina headed up to the trucks to get sandwiches made.

"George, will you please have the kids get out of the water and dry off in about 5 minutes so they are ready for lunch when we get back?"

"No problem Sweetie."

Maggie and Katrina came back about 15 minutes later carrying sandwiches. "Lunch is here, we have sandwiches & either potato or tortilla chips. Katrina said.

"Clara, will you please grab the fruit & the salsa out of the cooler for me?"

"Yeah mom will." Clara said with a sigh.

"Oh Clara you act like I asked you to run back to the trailer to get them. It's only five feet to the cooler." she looked over at Katrina and smiled.

"See what you get to deal with in a few years."

They all sat down and ate their sandwiches. Joey and Steve ate theirs as quickly as possible because they wanted to get back in the water.

"Mom, can we get back in the water now? We are done with lunch."

"Steve, why don't you and Joey wait a few minutes and let your stomachs settle."

"But we are bored!"

George looked over at Steve. "Let your mom enjoy her lunch. Why don't you and Joey go build a sand castle."

"Fine, come on Joey let's go build a sand castle."

"Ok Steve, let's build one big enough for us to climb into."

"Apparently they think we are going to be here all summer," Clara said.

"As long as it keeps them happy and busy for the day I'm fine with it," Maggie said.

32

It had been about an hour since reinforcements had arrived to help search for Rob & Jake. They had set up a base camp and Jerry, a Sheriff's deputy, would be manning the basecamp radio while the ten Search and Rescue members split into three teams. Four members would search with Gabe following the creek down where they had lost the tracks that they were following. Jim's team had three additional members that would be climbing up the hillside looking for tracks and using binoculars and a small drone to search from above. The final three Search and Rescue members would be going with Deputy Tim Daniels and they were going to go to start searching from the camp spot and make circles getting bigger and bigger looking for any signs that may have been missed.

Gabe took his team, Mark, Nancy, Bob, & Gary, and headed down to the creek. They slowly walked following the trail of markers making sure they didn't step on any of the tracks as they went. When they got to the last marker they made a circle around the marking to see if anyone could see which way the trail went. After making a full loop they confirmed that there was not a trail to follow, whatever had been being dragged along the ground must have been picked up. As they started towards the creek in the bottom of the ravine Gabe looked over his left shoulder and saw that Jim & his team were now in place to monitor the canyon as well as fly the drone over the canyon looking for any evidence.

Jim looked over at Ron, Joleen and Blake, the Search and Rescue members.

"Alright Ron & Joleen put the drone in the air and see if you can spot anything. Blake I need you to keep an eye out and let me know if you see any movement. It's possible that Gabe and his team might spook something up out of the canyon."

Gabe waved up at them and then went into the trees. The bottom of the canyon was full of Aspens and thick brush and Jim's team wouldn't be able to see them once they were in it. When Gabe and his team made it down close to the creek he stopped the team to make sure they knew to walk very carefully ensuring that they didn't step on any of the evidence. They all walked carefully down to the creek and Gabe showed them the footprints and the marks that looked like heels being dragged through the mud. They could see the footprints and the heel marks go into the water and then they couldn't see them again.

"Alright Mark & Bob, I want you to go to the other side of the creek and follow it down. Nancy & Gary, I want you to stay on this side of the creek. I'm going to walk down the creek. Make sure we all stay within sight of each other. I would like us to try and stay in line as much as possible, that way if any of us see something we need to investigate we can make sure we are checking the entire sight of the creek with minimal disturbances."

The four of them got in a line and started their search down the creek. They continued down trying to stay as close to each other as possible, but there were spots where the brush was so thick on the banks that the searchers would have to go around it. Gabe got to a point where the brush got really thick over he was just about to get out when he noticed some of the branches over the creek were broken. "Everyone stop, get in line with me and mark the location. I see a few bent and broken branches over the creek. I want you to circle the area looking for any signs."

After about fifteen minutes of searching and coming up with no other signs they decided to continue searching down the creek bed.

Gabe decided the brush was too thick over the creek so he got out and walked along the shore with Mark & Bob for about 100 feet. At this point the creek widened a little bit and little bit and the brush cleared off. All the searchers stopped on both sides and Gabe back tracked up the creek to where the brush was thick again. He could tell something big had come through the brush based on the broken branches. He took some pictures and marked the spot on his GPS and then continued back to where the rest of the team was.

"Alright guys let's take a little break before we continue."

All of them were thirsty so no one argued.

Back at the camp spot Tim and his team had completed their search without finding much evidence. It was almost two in the afternoon and although they hadn't seen signs that Rob & Jake had gone down the trail that led to the lake they decided they would start hiking it anyways in hopes that they would see them hiking back to the car. Tim headed off to Jerry's truck to let him know his plan but Jerry had another idea.

"Tim why don't you and Dave go hike the trail to the lake and Ben & Kevin can drive down to the lake and meet you. That way if they are walking along the road you won't miss them. At that point you can meet up with them and decide what your plan is but I would like to leave two of you at the truck in the parking lot and two of you to go hike the trail. If you haven't seen any sign of them a mile past the parking lot turn around and come back. I don't see much reason to search past there."

"You're the boss Jerry, we will be back in a couple of hours. I will keep you updated on the radio."

"Thanks Tim."

Tim & his team split up and went on their way.

33

"Is everyone ready to head back to camp?" George asked?

"It is just after three and we need some time to heat up the coals for the dutch ovens if we want to eat dinner at six."

"NO, we are having fun!" the kids yelled in unison.

"George, why don't you take our truck and go back with Mike & your Dad and the rest of us will leave in about an hour in Mike & Charles trucks." Maggie said.

"Sounds fine to me, do you want us to take the coolers?" George replied.

"You can take the food cooler back to camp. Will you please just put the drink cooler in the back of Mike's truck so we still have access to them?"

"Yeah, no problem. Alright Dad and Mike you heard the boss let's go."

They grabbed the coolers and walked the trail back to the trucks. They loaded the coolers up and jumped into George's truck. As they were headed down the road they noticed a Sheriff's truck slowly headed towards the lake.

Mike looked over at George, "I wonder if they found those boys?"

"I'm not sure, I would have thought so by now. They sure are driving slow like they are looking for something though."

"What are you guys talking about?" Charles asked.

They told him the story about the wreck and the missing students.

"Is that why you looked a little panicked when you found me George? You thought I had been eaten by some bear didn't you?" Charles said with a laugh.

"I was starting to get a little nervous Dad but I was more worried about you tripping and hitting your head on something."

"Good hell you act like I'm a feeble old man!"

"Well Dad, you are in your 70's."

"I know but I'm just as spry as when I was in my twenties go ahead and ask your mom." Charles winked at Mike.

"Ugh Dad, too much information." Mike said laughing.

They continued their drive and pulled into their camp at a little after four. They looked over at the camp chef's and they were knocked over.

"Those god damn cows have been in our camp!" Charles said.

"Hopefully nothing is broken." Mike replied.

They got out of the truck and headed over to the campsite. As they got over to Mike's camp chef they could tell one of the legs had been bent. "Damn it he said, I don't know how we are going to cook with it now."

"You can use one of the legs for my camp chef, I haven't even got it out of the trailer," Charles replied.

"Dad, you & Mike get his camp chef setup and start some coals. I'm going to go walk around the campsite and see if I can find out where those cows are. I would like to chase them off so they don't come back during the night."

"Alright be careful George, you know how temperamental those cows can be if they have a calf with them."

George headed off down the main walking trail that came into their camp, it was the same trail the boys had scared Clara on the day before. As he walked he kept looking for any signs of the cows but there were none to be seen. George continued to walk, he entered a pine tree grove, the same patch the boys had seen an animal the day before. He looked down at the ground and noticed some animal tracks but he couldn't quite tell what they were. He took a picture of them and then continued walking down the trail. After walking for another ten minutes or so without seeing any signs of the cows he decided to turn around. As he got close to the pines he happened to look over to his left and there was a piece of black fur hanging off a wild rosebush.

"I wonder what this is from?" he thought to himself.

George grabbed the fur and looked at it, he couldn't tell what type of animal it was from but he knew his dad probably could figure it out. He stuck it in his pocket and continued down the trail. As he got closer to the camp he could smell the charcoal burning and knew that the rest of the group should be back at any minute. George walked back into camp but didn't see anyone, he looked over at Mike's trailer and could see Charles & Mike both in the trailer getting dinner ready. George walked over to the back of the truck, opened the cooler and grabbed three beers out of it. He then headed over to help the others prepare dinner. He walked into the trailer and showed his dad and Mike the hair he had found.

"What type do you think it is dad?"

"I'm not sure it kind of looks like bear fur, but it could be the undercoat of a badger as well, maybe even a wolverine. There aren't very many around but it could be one. How far off the ground was it?"

"It was only six inches or so off the ground and stuck in a wild rose bush."

"My guess would be that it is from a badger that is shedding its under coat after winter."

"Yeah that would make sense. Let's get dinner cooking, then I want to show you a picture that I took on my walk."

They got the pizza's made and thrown into the dutch ovens. They then carried the dutch ovens outside and placed coals on top of them.

"Alright George, show us your pictures and then I will start the camp chef so we can cook the garlic bread in the pizza oven," Mike said.

George pulled out his phone and showed them the tracks that he saw near the pine grove. "What do you think those are from?" George asked.

"I'm not sure, they look almost like human prints but with long claws." Mike said.

"It's tough to tell, but they almost look like bear prints to me," Charles said.

"I guess that would make sense based on the hair I found. Do you think that is what knocked Mike's camp chef over?"

"It's possible, but it won't come around now that we are here. We best just lock our coolers and food items up tonight so it doesn't come back."

Around the same time that George was showing the others the pictures, the rest of the family was finishing packing up at the lake. They had the coolers and the chairs loaded up and just had to reign in the kids. Grandma had stayed back to watch them finish playing in the water while Katrina, Maggie, & Clara loaded things up in the truck.

"I will go back and grab Gloria and the kids if you guys want to stay here," Katrina said.

"Oh we will walk down with you, Clara and I don't mind. I would like to get one last look at the lake anyway."

They headed down the trail and when they got to the beach Gloria had the kids dried off and wrapped in towels.

"How did you manage to wrangle them all by yourself Gloria?" Katrina asked.

"Oh Grandma's have their tricks. I offered them cookies and ice cream after dinner."

"Isn't that what's for desert Grandma?" Clara asked.

"Yes but they don't know that." Gloria said as she winked at Clara.

"Alright everyone let's start heading back. We are already about thirty minutes late." Maggie said.

They all walked down the trail and climbed into the trucks. Joey, Steve & Marie rode with Gloria and Maggie, Katrina, and Clara rode in George & Maggie's truck. As they were leaving the parking lot Katrina noticed that a Sheriff's truck was waiting by the trail head that went back into the cliffs above the lake. The Sheriff's deputies in the trucks didn't look too concerned but it looked like they were waiting for someone.

"I wonder why they are sitting up here?" Joey asked.

"I'm not sure Joey, maybe they are watching for speeders leaving the parking lot." Gloria said.

They continued down the road and after about 45 minutes they made it back to camp. When they pulled in the three men were sitting in their chairs around the dutch ovens enjoying themselves.

"I think we got the short end of the stick ladies," Katrina said.

"Why do you say that Aunt Katrina?" Clara asked.

"Oh I'm just teasing, it just looks like the men have had a nice relaxing hour or so."

Maggie parked her truck and Gloria pulled in behind her. They all climbed out of the trucks as the three men came over to help unload the truck.

"How was the rest of your afternoon at the lake?" George asked.

"GREAT!" Joey & Steve yelled.

George walked over and gave Maggie a kiss and then grabbed the cooler out of the truck.

Mike & Charles helped carry the chairs out of the truck and took them over by the fire pit.

Katrina walked over to Mike and rubbed his shoulders.

"How much longer until dinner is ready?"

"Oh probably about 15 minutes."

"Ok, I'm going to go get changed, Marie & Joey, why don't you get out of your swimsuits and put some clothes on."

"Ok mom," they said in unison.

"Make sure you put the ones you wore around the fire last night so you don't get another pair smoky."

Maggie and Clara were walking over to their trailer and Maggie told Steve to go do the same thing. He put down the stick he was playing with and headed over to their trailer. Mike went over and started his camp chef, he needed to heat it up so he could cook the garlic bread. Once everything was ready and the kids had changed their clothes they all sat down for dinner.

After they were finished Maggie and Katrina went into Katrina's trailer and made margaritas. They carried them out and gave all of the adults sitting around the campfire one.

"Thank you dear." Gloria said.

"Mike, when do you want to put the camp chef and food away?" George asked.

"Let's finish the margaritas and then we can clean up. As long as we have it done before it gets dark it won't be a pain in the ass."

"Why are you putting the food stuff away? It should be fine." Gloria commented.

"Well we think there may be a bear visiting our camp," Charles said.

"Why would you think that?" Maggie asked.

George told her about the fur and tracks that he had seen as well as the camp chef being knocked over when they got back to camp.

"It's nothing to worry about Maggie, I'm sure the bear is gone, besides the way Gloria snores she will scare away anything that decides to come around at night," Charles said.

"CHARLES," Gloria said.

George tried to reassure his wife, but after the scare this morning with the kids and then the other camp that was torn up he had a hard time. Maggie was concerned about the possibility of a rogue bear wandering around and about her kids going anywhere outside of the camp.

Mike stood up "Alright, I'm going to go get the dinner stuff cleaned up. Katrina do you want to help me?"

"Sure dear." Katrina swallowed the rest of her margarita and stood up.

Katrina and Mike went over and cleaned off the camp chef and started packing it up so it wouldn't get knocked over again. George asked Clara to help clean up as well so the both of them grabbed the dutch ovens and headed into the trailer to get them clean out.

Maggie and Gloria sat watching the kids play catch with the frisbee Joey had brought.

"Are you ladies ready for me to start a fire?" Charles asked.

"Sure, you may as well get it going while there is some daylight left and before it starts to get cold. I'm going to go mix up another batch of Pina Colada, do you two want one?" Maggie asked.

Gloria smiled and said "That would be great dear, do you want me to go ask Mike & Katrina?"

"No, I'm sure they will want one, I will make a big batch."

Maggie headed to the trailer to help Clara finish washing the dishes and to make the drinks. After she was done her & George came out carrying the six drinks and handed them out.

Just as Katrina was sitting down Steve came running over, "Grandma can we have cookies & ice cream now?"

"Steve, why don't you let Grandma sit for a few minutes and rest." Maggie said.

"Oh, it's fine. Clara, will you come help me and we will dish up the ice cream and the cookies for you kids?"

"Sure Grandma."

Soon they came out carrying bowls full of ice cream and cookies for the kids. They all were able to sit around the fire and relax.

34

Rob woke up and laid there for a minute remembering where he was. He didn't know if he had been asleep for ten minutes or ten hours, but he did feel a little bit better other than he was shivering from the cold breeze that was still blowing in the tunnel. The last thing he remembered was being tired and leaning against the wall, he must have tipped over because while his back was against the wall his head was on the ground. He slowly sat up waiting for the throbbing headache to return. To his pleasant surprise the headache didn't seem quite as bad. He decided he would take the tunnel leading to the left since he could feel air flow in it. He started crawling slowly through the dark trying to keep his shoulder next to the wall, he didn't know what lay in front or to the side of him. Every time he crawled forward he would reach out with one hand and touch the floor in front of him as well as to his left to make sure he hadn't reached a ledge.

After crawling for a while he came to a point where he thought he could see a little bit of light coming out of the floor ahead. He hurried his crawl up a bit. He reached the spot where he could see the light, it was coming from behind a rock that was roughly the size of a suitcase. "There is no way I'm going to be able to move this rock," he thought. He tried to push the rock with his hand to no avail. He sat there thinking of what to do. He tried to push again but it still wouldn't budge. He then decided he would try to pull the rock away from the wall. This was a risky plan because it was possible the rock may fall on him or if he got it away from the wall and it fell back it may crush his fingers in the process.

Rob decided that it was worth the risk and he would take the chance. He stood up and pulled as hard as he could. The rock started to pull away but Rob's finger slipped and the rock fell back against the wall. He decided he would try again. This time he steadied his legs and his back. His plan was to pull the rock and when it was getting ready to tip he would jump to the side of the rock. He counted down to get himself prepared. 3.....2......1 and he pulled. The rock came away from the wall and he could feel its momentum carrying it away from the wall. As soon as it started to tip the other direction he jumped back towards the wall and the rock fell to the ground with a loud thud that reverberated through the tunnel. Rob sat there catching his breath. After a minute he crawled over to the crack that the light was shining through. He peaked down through the crack and could see that there was a cavern below him lit with small lamps that lined a walking path and stair rail. "I've seen this place before," he thought to himself.

"That's Lakota cave!" he said out loud. He remembered coming up here with the Boy Scouts over ten years ago. He remembered the dim lit walking path as well as the stalactites and stalagmites that he could see. He was very excited about this as he knew that during the summer months there were multiple tours everyday that came through the tunnel. He would just need to wait for the next tour to come through and yell for help. The only problem was he didn't know what day or time it was. It could be five minutes or fourteen hours until the next tour came through. He decided he would just have to be patient and wait for the next tour. There was no way he was going to move away from this spot now and risk getting lost even more than he already was.

35

It was just after 6pm and Terry was headed home. As was usual for a summer shift it had run late. He was going to go home and have dinner with Joselyn and then head up the canyon to see if he could be of any assistance to the Search and Rescue team. Just as he was pulling into the driveway his phone began to ring. It was a number that he vaguely recognized but could remember who it belonged to. He put his car into park and hit the answer button on his cell phone.

"Hello"

"Officer Johnson, it is Trevor Silverton"

That is why I recognized it, he thought. He remembered writing the number down during their meeting at the hospital.

"Hi Trevor, how are things going?"

"They are great!" he said. Becky had woken up and while she was still very weak she was able to talk.

"That is great news! Do you think I could come down and talk to her to try and find out what happened?"

Trevor sat silently for a few seconds.

"Yes you can, she is very weak but as long as it isn't stressing her that should be fine."

"I'm getting ready to go to dinner with my wife, do you mind if I stop by afterwards and get a statement from her?"

"That is fine with us as long as she is awake, she still needs her rest."

"I understand, I will be at the hospital in about an hour to get her statement. Thanks for calling me Trevor."

Terry hung up the phone and hurried into the house.

"Hi sweetie, how was your day?" Joselyn asked.

"It was busy but I just got really good news! Becky has woken up and her parents said they were ok with me coming down and getting a statement."

"Does that mean our dinner date is off for the night?"

"Absolutely not, I told them I would stop by afterwards and get Becky's statement. I just need to call the Sheriff real quick and give him an update."

Terry went and grabbed a coke out of the fridge and sat down at the kitchen table. He called the Police Chief and let him know that he would be stopping by the hospital for the statement if he was ok with that. After he got his approval he called the Sheriff and let him know about Becky as well as the fact that he wouldn't be able to go help the Search and Rescue team. The Sheriff thanked him for going and getting the statement and said they would be calling off the search for the night once it got dark. They didn't even know if someone was actually in trouble or not so they weren't risking continuing to search in the dark.

Terry then went and climbed in the shower. When the warm water hit his body he could feel the tension leave. He hadn't realized how much it had built up in his shoulders.

"Babe, are you about done? I'm getting hungry!"

"Yeah I'm just finishing up."

Terry climbed out of the shower and dried off. He decided he would ask Joselyn if they could stop by the hospital on their way to dinner. That way he had a better chance of catching Becky while she was awake. She knew he would be thinking about it the whole time that they were at dinner so she decided to go along with it. They headed out the door and left for the hospital. Terry decided to call Trevor on the drive over to make sure he was ok with them stopping by right now. Becky's family was fine with him stopping by right now while she was still awake. Trevor told Terry that he spoke to her about what had happened and she was very concerned about Rob & Jake. Terry knew he didn't have much information to give her but perhaps if she could remember what happened while she was up the canyon it would help.

When Terry & Joselyn arrived at the hospital Joselyn told Terry that she would wait either in the car or outside on the bench. She didn't want to go into the hospital and overwhelm Becky. Terry walked into the ICU and into Becky's room. When he saw her she looked like she had been in a fight with Mike Tyson and was very pale from her blood loss.

"Hi Becky, how are you?"

"Never been better," she said with a hint of a smile, her voice sounded very weak but at least she had a sense of humor.

"Have you found Rob & Jake yet?"

"No but they are searching, we haven't found any signs of foul play yet. The Search and Rescue will continue to search until dark and then they will start again in the morning. Can you tell me what happened last night?"

Becky started into her description of the night's events as best she could remember.

"Ok here is what I remember: After I got off the phone with you I decided I couldn't just sit around and wait to find out if Rob was in trouble or not. I drove over to his apartment complex and drove around the parking lot. I couldn't see his car so I decided to go knock on the door and see if Rob or Jake were home. After they didn't answer I tried to call again but nobody picked up. I then decided I would drive up the canyon and see if I could find them.

When I got up to where we had camped I found Rob's car. At first I was relieved because I thought maybe they were just really tired and fell asleep in the car. I got out of my car and walked up to Rob's car to see if they were in it but nobody was in it. This is when I started to get concerned because Rob's doors were unlocked and he never left them unlocked. I started calling out for him but I never heard a response. I went back to my car and grabbed my flashlight and headed back to Rob's car. I opened the door and looked inside to see if I could find anything that would let me know where they were. I then decided I would turn on the headlights so I could see better. That is when I saw something shiny laying on the ground by the pine trees. I walked over and realized that it was Rob's gun. I picked it up and got really scared because I knew he wouldn't have just left it lying on the ground."

"Wait so that wasn't your gun we found in your car?"

"No, that was Rob's gun, he was very proud of it and I didn't want it to get lost or stolen and I also wanted the protection.

"Ok so that clears up one question we had. Please proceed with your story."

Terry knew he needed to ask her about the casings in the car but decided to wait until the end of the story.

"I called out for Rob again and then decided I needed to go get help so I jumped in my car and headed down the canyon. I was coming around a corner and there was a deer and fawn in the roadway. They seemed spooked but I'm not sure what spooked them. Anyway I swerved to miss them and ended up crashing. After that I really don't remember much other than my head hurting and waking up in the hospital."

"I do have one last question for you Becky. When they were cleaning up your car they found two shell casings in the car. Did you pick those up?"

Becky sat there for a minute. Terry & Trevor could tell she was trying to remember how they had got there.

"I don't remember right now. Maybe I picked them up off the ground."

"Thank you for speaking with me Becky, I really appreciate it. I'm going to go submit this report and let the Sheriff know about the gun and where you found it. If you remember where you got the casings from please have your Dad call me. I'm more concerned for Rob & Jake than I was before. I will make sure your dad is updated with anything we found out so he can share it with you."

Becky nodded her head and closed her eyes telling the story had taken a lot of energy out of her and she needed to sleep. Trevor walked Terry out of the hospital and thanked him for being so concerned about Becky.

Terry then walked over to the bench where his wife was sitting and told her the story.

"I'm guessing you need to make a call before we go to dinner."

"Sorry sweetie, it will be quick I promise."

He then dialed the Sheriff's number to let him know what he had found out.

36

It was almost six and all of the search teams had been out longer than they expected. Tim's team had finished searching the upper trails and hadn't seen anything. Jim's group had searched the hillsides on foot and with the drone but couldn't find any sign of Rob or Jake. The most exciting thing they had seen was Gabe's team spook a herd of 10 elk out of the creek. They were all exhausted and they were waiting for Gabe's team to get back from their search.

Gabe's team had the most fruitful search of the day. They followed the creek for roughly three miles until it crossed a four wheeler trail. Every so often they could see drag marks throughout the creek but could never make out what was being dragged and what was dragging it. They stopped at the four wheeler trail for a break and then continued their search for another half a mile. After that they decided to turn around because they hadn't seen any drag marks since they crossed the trail.

Gabe had radioed Jim and asked him to meet at the trailhead which was at the Fredericks Basin turnoff. If they walked the four wheeler trail it would only be two miles down a well used trail which was a heck of a lot better than bushwhacking all the way back to where the headquarters was set up.

When they arrived at the trailhead the searchers sat down for a well needed break.

"Jim should be here any minute, so don't get too comfortable." Gabe said.

When Jim showed up he got out and asked how the search went. He asked if they had found any more evidence of what had happened. Gabe told him about the rest of the search and how the tracks seemed to end at the four wheeler trail.

"Do you think they were kidnapped and driven away on a four wheeler?" Jim asked Gabe.

"No I don't think so, I don't know how anyone would be able to carry someone through that brush by themselves. I'm still not one hundred percent positive that anything bad happened here, although that doubt is starting to go away."

"Yeah I agree with you I think these boys would show up back to their car by now. I still don't know how both of them could have been attacked by something without putting up a fight. I would have thought we would have seen more evidence of a struggle. Let's head back to headquarters, the Sheriff sent up some food and drinks for us all."

"Are we planning on searching all night?" Mark asked.

"No, the Sheriff is going to call us off at dark, unless we find significant proof that someone is seriously in danger." Jim responded.

When they arrived back at the campsite there was pizza and sandwiches waiting for them. Gabe walked over and grabbed a Coke out of the cooler and then loaded up his plate with chips, a slice of pepperoni pizza, & a turkey sandwich. He sat down and ate his food while trying to think of where the boys could have possibly gone. He had all but lost hope on the fact that the boys were just out on a hike and hadn't made it back yet.

Jim walked over to Gabe just as he was finishing up eating. "Hey Gabe, I just got a message that we need to go call the Sheriff as soon as possible."

"Did he find out information on the boys?"

"I don't know, it was just relayed that he wanted us to go call him."

They both walked over to Jim's truck and he pulled out his satellite phone. They didn't use these very often due to the cost, but they both thought this was a valid reason to use it. When they called the Sheriff told them the story Becky had relayed to Terry. He also told them about the gun lying on the ground and Becky picking it up.

"Did she give him a reason for the shell casings to be in her car?"

"No, she couldn't remember if she picked them up or how they got there. Terry said it looked like she truly couldn't remember. He didn't think she was holding information back."

"So it looks like we need to continue the search for the Sheriff?" Gabe asked.

"I think it would be best, it looks like something nefarious may have happened up there and we need to get to the bottom of it. I will send up reinforcements to monitor the area so you guys can come home and get some rest. I will also send up a helicopter tonight so they can try and get a better view and maybe find the boys with their thermal vision goggles."

"Ok thanks Sheriff." Gabe said.

"Well Jim, it looks like we have plans for the night."

"It sure does, no way in hell am I going home now."

They walked back over to the campsite and relayed the information from the Sheriff to the rest of the team. They decided that they needed to start a more detailed grid search, so they started mapping out grid coordinates for the search.

37

Terry and Joselyn were eating at a local steakhouse and they were waiting on dessert when Terry's phone began to ring. He looked down at the phone number and realized it was the office. He decided to ignore the call for now and just focus on the time with his wife. He had been busy at work for the last couple of weeks so they hadn't had a lot of time together. Immediately after the first call ended his phone began to ring again, it was the office again.

"Honey you better just answer and see what they need. What if it has to do with the case you have been working on."

Terry sighed and answered his phone. It was his boss calling.

"I need you to meet the Sheriff & I at the office as soon as possible. It is regarding the kids that you took the police report from yesterday."

"Did they find the boys?"

"Well one of them possibly. Meet me at the office and I will update you."

"Ok boss I will see you in a little bit."

Terry hung up the phone and told his wife what the Police Chief had told him. They had the dessert packed up in a to-go box and Terry took Joselyn home. He gave her a kiss and headed to the office.

As Terry was driving to the Police station his phone began to ring again. He looked at the caller ID and it was Trevor's number.

He picked up his phone, "Hello."

"Officer Johnson?"

"Yes"

"It's Trevor, I think you need to come down to the hospital. Becky just woke up in a panic, she said she needed to talk to you immediately. We tried to get her to calm down but she won't. She keeps saying she knows what happened to the boys."

"Alright, I'm headed to the station, but I will stop at the hospital first so I can talk to her."

He hung up his phone, made a turn down Blossom St. and headed towards the hospital.

When he arrived at the hospital he saw Trevor standing at the front doors waiting for him. They walked back into the hospital and down the corridor to the ICU. When they walked in Becky was sitting up and looked very scared and very weak. Sitting in a chair next to her was Becky's mom Diana.

"This is my wife Diana, Becky's mom."

"Nice to meet you." Terry said as they shook hands.

"Diana got here about an hour ago, she had been on a business trip and was in the Orlando Airport when we heard about the accident." Trevor said.

"Becky, you Dad said you needed to talk to me, what is going on?"

"I remember why the bullets are on the car floor and I think I know what happened to Rob & Jake."

"Ok Becky if this is any sort of confession I do need to read you your rights first."

"WHAT? No this isn't a confession I didn't do anything wrong."

"Sorry for upsetting you, I just didn't know where you were going to be leading us after your last sentence. Please continue."

"After I wrecked I was sitting in the car and could see a big dark shadow in the trees, I'm guessing that is what scared the deer onto the road. Anyways it kept moving around and moving closer. I yelled at it but it wouldn't go away so I pulled out the gun and shot at it. I don't think I hit it, but I must have been close because it took off running."

"Wow that must have been very scary Becky, I will send an officer to check for blood in the morning just to confirm that you didn't hit it. If you did, maybe we can find out what it was. Can you tell me how this pertains to Rob & Jake?"

"I think that the creature that tried to pull Jake away the night before took them, I think that is what I shot at."

"Why do you think that?"

"I don't know, I just had a dream about them looking for the phone and getting attacked and the creature in my dreams fit Jake's description."

"Thank you for calling Becky, I need to get to the police station so I can relay the information and we can get to the bottom of this. Nice to meet you Diana."

Terry shook her hand and walked out of the room with Trevor.

"Do you think her story is accurate?" Trevor asked.

"I think it is accurate as to why she shot into the trees, I have no doubt she was terrified. I'm doubting the rest of it as far as the monster that attacked Jake & Rob was also following her down the canyon, but I won't discount it and we will look into it.

Terry thanked Trevor again as he climbed into his cruiser and headed for the station. When Terry walked into the Police station he saw the Police Chief and Sheriff in the Police Chief's office. He walked in and greeted them. He apologized for being so late and told them about needing to stop by the hospital. He also relayed Becky's story to them.

The Sheriff then told Terry what had transpired so far in the day as to the search for Rob & Jake. He told him about the searches that were still on going and then he told him about the most recent update to the story.

"About an hour ago we received a call from a man named Dillon that worked as a guide at Lakota Cave. The caller was frantic that there was someone stuck in a chamber above one of the large rooms in the cave. Dillon had stated that the individual had no idea how he had arrived in the cave and he was injured and cold. The individual's name that is stuck in the cave is Rob."

Terry's eyes go big.

"Is it the Rob we are searching for? Was Jake with him? Had they gone hiking and gotten lost in the cave?"

"We don't have any other details right now, I am getting ready to have a search party go up and find out where this hiker entered the cave. One would assume that this is the same Rob since it would be unlikely that there would be two missing."

"Lakota Cave is a LONG ways away from Aspen Grove. I would guess ten miles away as the crow flies."

"Yes it is, which is why we are concerned. How did Rob get from one location to the other?"

Just then the Sheriff's phone rang.

"It's Gabe, let me answer this so we can update him."

"Gabe, just the man I was wanting to talk to."

"Sheriff, what can I do for you? The deputy manning our radio contact came down and said you needed to talk to me immediately. I assumed it was urgent since we talked just an hour ago."

"Yes Gabe I did need to talk to you. The Police Chief and Officer Terry Johnson are sitting here with me. About an hour ago we received a call from a man named Dillon that worked as a guide at Lakota Cave. The caller was frantic that there was someone stuck in a chamber above one of the large rooms in the cave. Dillon had stated that the individual had no idea how he had arrived in the cave and he was injured and cold. The individual's name that is stuck in the cave is Rob."

"Sheriff, that doesn't make sense, how would Rob get from Aspen Grove over to Lakota Cave?"

"The caller said that Rob claimed he didn't know how he got in there. I'm requesting that you & Jim head over to Lakota Cave and talk to Rob. We need to find out how he got into a chamber above Lakota Cave. As far as I know there is only one entrance."

"Ok Sheriff we will head over there. Whom do I need to talk to?"

"The caller's name is Dillon, he is the guide working up there."

"Ok, we will head over right now, it is probably going to take us over an hour to get there from here."

"That is fine, Dillon was on the last tour of the day when they heard Rob calling for help. He has stopped all access to the cave and will wait for you to get up there. I'm going to have Terry continue to work on the case here in town and see what he can find out."

"Ok thanks Sheriff I will contact you when we get over to Lakota Cave."

"One more thing, Terry has more information for you as far as the gun in Becky's car."

Terry told the story to Gabe and it was decided that they would go check out the location in the morning if they hadn't already found Rob & Jake.

The Sheriff hung up the phone and asked Terry if he was ok to continue to work the case once they had more details from Rob. Terry was ok with this. He was going to go home and talk to his wife and then he would be ready to do whatever he needed to do.

38

It was just starting to get dark in Fredericks Basin. Steve, Joey, Marie, & Clara were getting ready to play laser tag. Maggie had told them to stay within sight of the camp. They didn't want them wandering too far from camp after a possible bear could have been in their camp. The rest of the family was sitting around the fire enjoying the night.

"Mom, will you get my jacket? I'm getting cold," Marie called out.

"Yes dear I will, Joey do you want yours as well?

"No thanks mom."

Katrina headed for the trailer to grab the jackets, she looked up on the hillside and smiled. She could see a deer with two fawns grazing on the grass up on the hillside. She walked into the trailer and grabbed the kids jackets. She also made sure the heater was set to kick on at 65 degrees. Last night when she came in the trailer to get the kids ready for bed it was quite cold.

When she came out she told the kids to pause their laser tag game so Marie could get her coat on.

"Mom, I told you I didn't want mine." Joey said.

"I know but you will eventually and I didn't want to have to go back into the trailer to get it once I sit down. I will just put your jacket over here on the table. Now go back and have fun."

Katrina then went back over to the fire and asked if anyone needed anything. Mike & George wanted a beer so she walked over to the cooler and grabbed two.

"Thanks Katrina," George said as she handed the beer to him.

"Maggie just headed into the trailer to make margaritas, she said she would bring you one out."

"That's nice of her, I probably better only have one tonight, I had heartburn last night and with there being a chance that a bear may visit our camp I don't know that I will sleep well tonight."

"Oh, it will be fine sweetie. Even if a bear does come into camp we will be in our trailers and a black bear isn't going to do much but smell around for food and head on his way." Mike said.

"I know it just makes me nervous having the kids outside playing after dark knowing there is a hungry bear in the area."

"I think that bear has left," Charles said.

"Oh yeah, what makes you think that dad?" George asked.

"Well black bears are known to be skittish animals and if there are humans around it will more than likely stay away. If it were a Grizzly bear I would be more concerned but I don't think a black bear is going to hunt any of us down."

"Yeah that's true," Mike said with a smile on his face.

"What are you smiling about Mike? You don't seem to be too concerned about our kids," Katrina said.

"It's not that. I was thinking about when George and I were kids and we went to Yellowstone as a family. We were driving down the road looking for animals and a bison jam slowed all of the cars down. We looked out the passenger side window and we saw two bears scurrying up a dead lodgepole pine tree trying to hide from the bison. It was the most entertaining thing we had seen on the trip. Bears are looked at as these big ferocious beasts and there they were climbing up a dead tree to hide from some bison."

"Ha ha, I do remember that," George said.

"We had just finished eating ice cream at the Tower Falls gift shop and were headed back to Mammoth I think."

"Yeah you are right. I can't believe you kids remember that I think you were only 7 & 9 at the time. Your mom was fit to be tied!

She was so concerned that our car was going to get rammed and trampled by a bison."

"Those bison were not happy about a bear being around; they looked like they were going to start ramming all of the cars in the road. That is the angriest I have ever seen a bison." Gloria said.

"I know darling, it was kind of unsettling to have that many bison around us."

Just then Maggie came out carrying six margarita's on a tray.

"I didn't know you guys were going to have a beer instead, I guess us ladies will just have to drink these." Maggie said as she was handing out the drinks.

"Oh I think we can handle both, I can't miss out on one of your homemade margaritas" Mike said.

39

The sun had been down only a few minutes when Gabe & Jim made it to the entrance of Lakota cave. They saw only one car in the parking lot and the light was on in the trailer. As they pulled up a man stepped out of the trailer and started walking over to them. They both got out of Jim's truck and greeted the man.

"Hi I'm Gabe, I'm with the Fish & Game and this is Jim he is a Sheriff's Deputy. I understand you made quite the discovery this evening."

"Ha, that is an understatement!"

"Hi I'm Dillon, one of the guides here at the cave and yes we made quite the discovery. When I first heard the voice I thought I was going crazy until some of the guests were also wondering where it was coming from."

"We would like to head into the cave if that is possible, I want to talk to this Rob guy and see what we can find out and see if he can give us any description on how he got into the cave so we can help him get out."

"Sure! We can head down there right now. Let me go grab a flashlight for the trail leading over to the cave entrance."

"I thought it was lit up?" Jim asked.

"The cave has lights in it but not the trail heading over to the cave. Normally we aren't walking over there in the dark."

Dillon walked back over to the little shed that had been made into an office and grabbed his flashlight. The three of them then headed down the half mile trail to the opening of the cave. As they got to the entrance Dillon turned off his flashlight and opened the door to the cave. The door was a slatted metal door that allowed bats to fly in and out but would keep people out.

"How far do we need to go before we will be at the spot you heard Rob speaking?" Gabe asked.

"We need to go about half way in so about one third of a mile"

They continued walking down into the cave for about twenty minutes until they came to the spot.

"Here is the spot we hear him calling from. I believe it is from that crack up there in the rock."

"ROB" Gabe yelled.

"Can you hear me? This is Gabe Campbell with Fish & Game."

At first there was silence and then they could hear a faint cry coming from the crack. It was gravely call saying "Help me"

"Rob, we are here to help you. Do you know how to get into the cave system you are in?"

"No, help me, something attacked me." Rob said in a strained voice.

"I know we need to figure out how you were brought over here to this cave. I'm not sure what attacked you."

"No something.... something attacked me a few minutes ago."

Rob's voice was very strained and they could tell he was in a lot of pain.

"You mean something is in the cave with you?"

"Yes, help me."

"Gabe I'm going to go out and call for help, stay here with Dillon and keep Rob talking. I'm going to go out of the cave and call for assistance. We have to get help over here immediately."

"Do you think going out on your own is such a good idea Jim?"

Jim looked over at Gabe. "We don't have a choice."

Jim then turned around and hurriedly started walking back up the trail to the entrance of the cave. He knew he would need to hurry out and make a call to get the rescue team brought over to the cave.

40

Terry pulled into his driveway and turned his car off. He didn't want to work this weekend but he knew he wouldn't be able to keep his mind off of the case anyways so he may as well help the best he could. He got out of his car and headed into the house. As he opened the door he saw Joselyn sitting on the couch.

"Hey sweetie, you made it home. What did you learn while you were at the office?"

"Gabe called in to the meeting and the Sheriff told us that they may have found Rob over near Lakota Cave. Gabe & one of the Sheriff's deputies are on their way over to Lakota Cave right now to find out what is going on."

"Do you have to go back to work?"

"No, not as of yet. The Police Chief asked me to work the case from down here once we have more information so right now I'm going to grab a drink and relax. Do you want anything?"

"Sure, maybe I will have a glass of wine and we can go sit on the deck. I will go grab a jacket while you are getting the drinks."

Terry walked into the kitchen and grabbed two wine glasses out of the cupboard. He then picked up a bottle of his homemade huckleberry wine and poured it into the two glasses. Joselyn walked into the kitchen and gave Terry a kiss on the cheek.

"Thanks for the wine."

They grabbed their glasses and walked out the back sliding door and sat down. Their patio faced east so while they were unable to see the sunset they could see the mountains turning a dull orange color as the sun's last rays touched the mountain. Terry took a sip of wine and stared up at the mountains thinking of how beautiful they were, yet knowing there was a not so beautiful scene playing out up in the same mountains.

41

Thirty minutes ago Jim had left Dillon & Gabe and headed toward the opening of the cave and he could now feel air coming in from the outside of the cave so he knew he was getting close to the entrance. He was starting to get tired, it had been quite a day starting with Becky's accident and continuing with the search for Rob which had then led them a mountain range away to Lakota Cave.

As he reached the entrance it was almost pitch black outside, he looked at his watch and saw it was almost ten. He knew the moon should rise in the next hour but being in the mountains meant that the time frame could be a little off. He turned on his flashlight and headed down the trail to his truck. As he walked down the trail the hairs on his neck started standing up, he felt as though something was watching him. He started turning around and shining his flashlight into the trees. He couldn't see anything so he thought to himself, *come on Jim keep it together, you are just tired from today you are being paranoid.*

Jim continued down the trail for a few more steps and heard something rustle in the bushes. He stopped immediately and shined his flashlight in the direction of the sound. The bushes rustled again and suddenly Jim found himself on the ground, his flashlight rolling down the hill. He felt a large animal on top of him that was trying to pin him down. He tried to fight his way free but couldn't get away. The beast grabbed his throat and began squeezing. Jim fought as hard as he could against the beast. He quit trying to pry the beast's hands off of his neck and decided to try another alternative knowing that if he didn't get loose soon he was a goner. He reached up and jammed his fingers into both of the beast's eyes. The beast's hands left Jim's neck and it stood up grabbing at its eyes and roaring in pain. Jim brought his knees to his chest and with all of his strength he kicked the beast sending it down the hill.

"What the hell is that," he thought.

Jim got up and started running down the trail again he knew he needed to make it back to his truck and call for help. He had made it about the length of a football field before he heard rustling in the bushes again.

"How in the hell did that thing cover so much ground so quickly? Are there two of them?" he thought.

He stopped and squatted down waiting to see the animal come out of the bushes. He saw the grass and branches moving roughly ten feet in front of him. He slowly pulled his gun out of his holster and waited. What in the hell is this thing, it wrapped its hands around my neck. He couldn't think of any animal other than an ape or chimpanzee that would be able to attack like this.

Ten seconds went by and everything went silent. Jim stood up and started looking around, his eyes had adjusted to the darkness so he was able to see a little better. He started slowly moving down the trail watching for any little movement or sound. After a few minutes he could see the parking lot and his truck. He let down his guard and started walking quicker knowing that if he could get to the truck he would be safe. He would be able to call for backup as well as use the lights to hopefully keep the beast at bay.

Jim was just 150 feet away from the parking lot when there was a big crash coming through the trees and Jim found himself on his back again, his gun flying out of his hand and into a bush as he hit the ground. The beast wasn't going to let him go this time it began pounding the back of Jim's head into the ground with such ferocity that he began blackout. Jim attempted to fight back but to no avail and soon he was lying lifeless on the trail. The beast stood up on two legs and looked down across its bulky frame into Jim's glazed over eyes. The creature grabbed Jim's legs and started dragging him into the brush.

Down in the cave Gabe & Dillon were trying to keep Rob awake and assure him that he was going to be okay. Gabe looked down at his watch, it was 10:30.

Jim should be at the truck by now and radioing for help, he thought.

"Rob are you doing okay up there? Jim should be getting to his truck now and calling for help so we can get more people over here to help search for the entrance to the cave system that you are in." Gabe said.

"Yeah I'm doing okay it is just very cold in here," Rob replied.

After a few minutes Rob began to scream. "Help, something is grabbing my leg and trying to drag me away."

Rob kicked blindly into the dark with his free foot, trying to get free of whatever was trying to grab him. Below all Gabe & Dillon could do was listen to what was happening and hope that Rob could fight off the animal. They heard a loud growl and then there was silence. "Rob, is everything okay?"

There was only silence.

Shit, Gabe thought.

They waited a few more minutes and called for Rob again but there was never a reply.

"Alright we aren't going to do much good down here if Rob is no longer at the hole, let's head out so we can meet up with the calvary and get this search under way." Gabe said.

Dillon didn't say anything, he just looked terrified. Gabe started to walk back out of the cave, he turned around and Dillon was just staring at the hole in the cave ceiling.

"Dillon, come on we need to get out of here so we can help Rob." Dillon nodded his head and they started walking to the entrance of the tunnel.

42

Over in Fredericks Basin the Jacobs family had been sitting around the campfire and eating smores. The kids had finished their laser tag game and were getting tired.

"Alright kids, it's time to get ready for bed," Maggie proclaimed.

"Ah come on Mom, we want to stay up a little later." Steve protested.

"No it has been a long day and it is time to get ready for bed, now finish your smore and go brush your teeth."

Katrina looked over at Joey & Marie and told them it was time to go get ready for bed as well. Neither of them argued as they were both exhausted from all of the adventures they had been on that day. Joey & Marie got up out of their chairs and gave their dad a hug. They then waved good night to the rest of the family and headed towards the trailer.

"Well I guess I better go help them get the beds ready and then I think I'm going to bed as well, I'm exhausted!" Katrina said.

Steve slowly ate his smore and then got up out of his chair, he walked around giving everyone a hug and telling them good night. After this he headed towards their trailer.

"Make sure you brush your teeth before you get in bed." Maggie said.

"I will."

The rest of the family sat around for a few more minutes before Gloria, Charles, Maggie, & Clara decided to head in for bed.

"Mike, you want one more beer?" George asked.

"Yeah I will have one more while this fire burns down and then I think I will hit the sack."

"Agreed, I'm exhausted. What are your plans for tomorrow?"

"I think we will just hang around camp tomorrow, maybe go for a little drive up the canyon and go for a hike." Mike said.

"That sounds like a good time, maybe we will join you."

"You're more than welcome too, I'm sure Joey & Marie would be happy if Steve and Clara came along."

They both sat there looking up at the stars and watching the moon rise over the mountain tops to the east. After they finished their beers they poured water over the fire and headed to bed.

43

It had taken Gabe & Dillon twenty minutes to get out of the cave. They had both been hiking as fast as they could so by the time they walked out of the cave they were both breathing hard. They stopped just long enough to turn their flashlights on.

"Alright Dillon you know this trail better than I do you lead the way."

Dillon gave Gabe a nod and started jogging down the trail. Gabe was following close behind.

As they came around a bend Gabe said in a hushed voice "Dillon stop right there."

Dillon stopped, turned around and saw Gabe looking down the hillside. As he walked back towards Gabe he looked down the hill and could tell something was lighting up the brush. "Dillon, did you notice that light on our way into the cave earlier?"

"No I didn't but it wasn't as dark so we may have missed it. Sometimes clients drop their flashlights after coming out of the cave and don't notice they are gone. Maybe that is where this one came from."

Gabe pulled a piece of bright yellow plastic out of his pocket and tied it to a tree.

"I'm marking this spot so if we need to come back to it we can. Alright let's get down the trail and ask Jim what the ETA is for our search crew."

After jogging the rest of the way to the parking lot they slowed down as they got to the pavement. They could tell that Jim was not in his truck and they didn't see him anywhere. "JIM" Gabe called out but didn't receive a response.

He tried to call out his name two more times but in return there was nothing but silence.

"I don't like the feeling of this, something isn't right" Gabe said.

"Do you think that Jim fell down the hillside where we saw the flashlight?" Dillon asked.

"It's possible, but we weren't very quiet while we were stopped on the trail. I would have thought he would have heard us and called out."

"Maybe we should go back and check, he could be hurt." Dillon stated.

"We left our radio's in Jim's truck since we knew we wouldn't be able to make a call from the cave, let's go call dispatch and request help. Once we have done that we can go search for Jim."

They walked over to Jim's truck and opened the door. Gabe grabbed a radio and realized it was dead. He then grabbed the other radio and tried to use it but it had died as well.

"Shit, he didn't put these back on the charging stations, they are dead and I don't have cell service."

"If you head up to the top of that knoll you can get cell service, that's where all of the employees go to make calls during the day." Dillon stated.

"Perfect, why don't you go into your shed and grab a rope in case we need to haul Jim out of the ravine. I will go call dispatch and see if they have heard from Jim."

Gabe started up the hill, it wasn't very far, maybe two hundred yards in total but it was steep. Gabe's legs and feet were on fire from all of the hiking he had already done today but he knew he had to push on if there was any chance of saving Rob and now possibly Jim.

Once Gabe got to the top of the hill he looked down at his cell phone, he had two bars of service. He dialed the dispatch number and Janice answered.

"Hi Janice it is Gabe, how are you doing?"

"I'm doing well Gabe, how is your search going?"

"We found Rob inside a cavern above Lakota cave and we need the search party over here to help us find the entrance. Has Jim called you?"

"No we haven't heard from Jim, wasn't he in the cave with you?"

"Yes, he was but once we found Rob I stayed in the cave to keep in contact with Rob and Jim came back to the truck to radio in. While we were waiting something attacked Rob and drug him off, so our tour guide Dillon and I came back to the truck so we could help organize the search party when they arrived. Janice I'm afraid that Jim may have slipped down the hillside and I need to go check. Will you please radio the search party that is up Aspen Grove and send them our way. Also once I head down the hillside I'm going to lose service again so will you please inform the Sheriff of what is going on and see if he can send more help?"

"You got it, I'm going to make the calls now, be careful Gabe."

"We will be, thanks Janice."

After hanging up the phone Gabe jogged back down the hillside into the parking lot. He walked over to the shed where he expected to see Dillon. The lights were off so he called out for Dillon.

"I'm over here," Dillon said.

Gabe shined his flashlight behind the shed and saw Dillon squatting behind a barrel.

"Why are you back there hiding in the dark?"

"Something big was moving over by the trailhead and I didn't have anything to protect myself?"

"Are you sure?"

"Yes I'm sure and it was something at least six feet tall because I could see its head above the brush, not to mention did you look in our shed? Something has torn it apart."

Gabe walked back to the front of the shed and opened the door, the inside had been trashed, something had came into the shed and pulled the maps off of the walls and destroyed the computer screen as well as overturned the bookshelves where the tour crew had kept their pamphlets and headlamps.

"Let's go sit in the truck and wait for help, I don't want to leave Jim out there but I feel we need to get the search crew lined up as soon as they arrive" Gabe said.

"I can wait here while you go back to look for Jim."

"I'm not leaving you by yourself after seeing what this place looks like and having a Sheriff's deputy missing."

While he didn't want to leave Jim out in the brush any longer than needed he also knew it was unsafe to have Dillon here alone and waiting for the crews to arrive so he sat in the driver's seat of Jim's truck and leaned his head back to rest a little bit before what he assumed would be a long night of searching.

44

Terry had just walked into the house to grab another beer and heard the call over the radio requesting that the search crews up Aspen Grove head to Lakota Cave. He was hoping that no one else had gotten hurt and hopefully they had found Rob. He started back out the door and then decided to grab his radio off the counter and bring it with him hoping he would be able to stay updated on what was going on. Part of him wanted to head up the canyon immediately and try to help out. Since he didn't have any details on the move from Aspen Grove to Lakota Cave he figured it would be best to stay in town in case he needed to follow up on anything that the searchers may need in town.

After a few minutes a call came in requesting any volunteer search and rescue personnel to head up the canyon. The request had stated that Gabe had spoken with Rob while in the cave and that a Sheriff's deputy may be injured after falling down a hillside. Terry sat in his chair staring up at the mountainside. He was torn on whether to stay down in town and work the case from this side or to head up the canyon and try to help his fellow officers.

"Terry, why don't you just call the Police Chief and ask him if he is ok with you heading up the canyon?" Joselyn asked.

"Because it is past 10:30 on a Friday evening, I don't want to bother him."

"Oh for hellsake's Terry you know damn well he is following the radio chatter just like you are. Just call him."

Terry reached over to the patio table and picked up his cellphone, it rang three times and went to his voicemail so Terry left a message telling the Police Chief that he had been listening to the radio and hear the call for all available volunteers to head up the canyon and wanted to know whether he wanted him to stay in town or if he could head up to help in the search.

After hanging up he looked over at Joselyn, "I told you he wouldn't answer."

"Well at least you left him a message and let him know you were ready. Now all you can do is wait for directions on what to do."

45

George had just climbed into bed and was reading a book when he started to hear the thwop thwop thwop of a helicopter flying overhead. He got out of bed, threw on a shirt and opened the door to the trailer at the same time that Mike opened his door to see what was going on. They could see a search light coming up the canyon with a helicopter flying only about three hundred feet off of the ground. They both stepped out of their trailers and watched the helicopter fly overhead and continue on up the canyon.

"I wonder what that was all about?" Mike asked.

"Hell if I know, it's odd that they would be flying that low up a canyon in the dark. I thought they may be searching for something but they were flying too fast to see whatever they were looking for."

"Well let's hope that is all the excitement for the night, I will see you in the morning," Mike said.

George waved back at him and went into the trailer.

"What was that about?" Maggie asked. George told her about the helicopter and reassured her that they were on their way up the canyon at a quick pace so there was nothing to worry about around their campsite.

Meanwhile over at Lakota Cave, Gabe could also hear the faint but unmistakable sound of a helicopter flying. After a few more minutes the sound began to get louder and soon Gabe and Dillon could see the search light from the helicopter coming up over the mountain top. Gabe climbed out of the truck and grabbed four bright LED road markers. He then popped his head back in the door and told Dillon to come help him.

"We need to set up these markers so the pilot knows where it is safe to land."

He pointed to two spots and told Dillon to go place the markers. It was only moments later when the helicopter was overhead and began its descent to land in the middle of the parking lot. After landing the engine was shut down and the pilot Tim and two Sheriff's deputies, Jared and Barry got out and headed over to talk to Gabe.

"What is going on Gabe?" Jared asked.

"I'm not sure. I just know that Jim is missing, the shed over here has been ransacked and we have to find the second entrance to the cave or Rob doesn't have a chance.

"Alright, I'm going to go back up in the helicopter with Tim and Barry is going to stay here with you."

"Sounds good, as soon as the search crew gets here we will split them up and start looking for Rob and Jim," Gabe replied.

Jared headed back toward the helicopter with Tim. They climbed inside and Tim took a couple of minutes to go over his checklist. Once he was done the helicopter slowly lifted off the ground and they were on their way to look for any possible heat sources that may help them find Jim or Rob.

Gabe introduced Barry to Dillon and then they pulled out a map and started marking grid points on it that they could use for search areas. Barry was going to oversee the team searching for Jim and Gabe would oversee the team searching for the entrance to the cave where they hoped to find Rob still alive.

"Alright Barry, I think that is about all we can do until the rest of the search crew arrives. I think we should walk down to where I saw Jim's flashlight and see if he is laying on the ground. We can leave a note for the search crews to start preparing their equipment and unless we find Jim we should be back shortly after they arrive."

"I'm all for heading out to see if we can find Jim, but why don't we leave Dillon here in the truck while we go out and search for Jim."

Dillon spoke up, "I don't think that is a good idea."

"We don't know what is out there so I think it would be best if you stayed here at the truck Dillon," Barry stated.

"Dillon, I will leave a shotgun here with you in the truck. Barry and I won't be gone long, forty five minutes at most. You will be safer sitting in a truck with a shotgun than you will be out on the trail with us."

"Ok, I guess I will stay."

Gabe grabbed a shotgun from behind the seat of Jim's truck and handed it to Dillon.

"Do you know how to shoot one of these?"

"Yes I have hunted before, I know how to use a gun."

"Alright, climb in the truck and lock the doors, we will be back soon. Don't use the gun unless you are in imminent danger. More than likely nothing will bother you while you're sitting in the truck."

Dillon nodded his head that he understood and climbed into the truck. He closed the door and locked it.

Gabe and Barry turned away and started walking towards the trailhead, both of them determined to find Jim and get him help. Their attention could then shift back to finding Rob. They turned on their flashlights and started walking down the trail looking for any signs. As they walked they came across a spot that looked like something had been dragged into the brush.

"It looks like something got drug into the bushes right here doesn't it Gabe?"

"Yeah it does, we didn't notice it when we were walking out to the truck. Let's mark the spot and we can add it to the search area when we get back from checking the location of the flashlight."

They tied a marker to a branch that was next to the trail and headed towards the spot where Gabe & Dillon had seen the flashlight. Once they arrived at the yellow marker that Gabe had tied they called out to Jim to see if they could get an answer. After calling out a few times and not hearing Jim they started to slowly walk down the steep bank.

When they arrived at the bottom they walked over to the flashlight but couldn't see Jim anywhere. They started to search the area near where the flashlight was found for any signs of Jim.

"Hey Gabe, you may want to come over here."

Gabe walked over to the spot where Barry was standing and shining his light on the ground.

"Shit" Gabe said.

On the ground was a small spot of blood and the same footprints that had been found on the ground near Rob's car.

"I think we have a problem here Barry, we need to get back to the truck and call for more backup. I think Jim may have been attacked by whatever the hell has been terrorizing people up here."

Barry nodded his head in agreement and went to grab Jim's flashlight and then thought against it.

"Gabe, I'm going to leave this here for evidence."

"Probably a good idea in case this turns into yet another crime scene."

They climbed up the hill and started back towards the parking lot on the dark trail. As they walked past the location of the drag marks that led into the brush Gabe hesitated wanting to go searching for Jim. He knew the smart decision was to go back to the parking lot and meet up with the search teams so he continued walking.

When they got back to the parking lot they saw five vehicles parked and eight searchers preparing their gear. Gabe looked over at the group and to his relief Dillon was out of the truck and looked to be in good spirits. Gabe walked over to the searchers and told them about the flashlight and what they had found. Barry pulled out his radio and called up to the helicopter team who was making a circular pass over the mountain side looking for any signs of life. He let Jared & Tim know what they had found and asked them to radio down to dispatch to send more help. After getting off of the radio with them he walked back over to the search teams. A few more searchers had shown up so now they were up to fifteen including Gabe & Barry.

"Hey Barry, I just had a thought. Would those thermal vision goggles show a difference between the outside air temperature and the air temperature of the cave entrance. It is a fairly warm evening and the air coming out of the cave would be cooler."

"I haven't ever used them before but I would think they would show the difference. Let me radio up to Tim & Jared and have them test it out on the main entrance to the cave that way we know."

Gabe radioed up to the helicopter team and they headed over towards the entrance. When they arrived they let Gabe know they could see a distinct difference in the air temperature readings. They now switched from looking just for heat coming off the bodies of the animals to also looking to see if they could find another entrance to the cave.

Gabe & Barry spoke for a few minutes and determined it would be best for Barry to take seven of the searchers and head out looking for Jim while Gabe and the other searchers planned out the search for Rob.

Gabe told Barry's team good luck as they headed off towards the trailhead. They were all hoping for the best, but knew if the drag marks were from Jim the night may have a gruesome ending.

46

Steve woke up to something outside of the trailer rummaging around in their supplies. He peaked out the window but didn't see anything. He walked over to the trailer door and opened it slowly so as to not wake anyone up. Steve looked around and didn't see anything but could hear something under the trailer. He thought about waking his dad up but then figured it was just a raccoon and he could scare it away.

Steve stepped out onto the ground and closed the door leaving it unlatched so it wouldn't wake anyone up. As he peaked under the trailer he could see a raccoon on the other side roaming around. He walked around the front of the trailer and toward where the raccoon was. As he got close the raccoon saw him and started running off towards the trees. Steve went and picked up the garbage that the raccoon had strung across the ground. As he stood back up and turned around he froze. Five feet away and blocking his path back to the trailer was a large what looked to be bigfoot standing in his way.

Steve screamed which seemed to startle the beast, but instead of running away it ran straight for Steve and grabbed him. The beast picked him up and ran straight for the hillside and into the trees. The last thing Steve saw as the beast carried him away was the lights coming on in the trailer.

When Maggie & George heard Steve scream they both sat straight up and turned the light on. George jumped out of bed and grabbed his gun from the closet. Maggie was already in the main room of the camper and saw Steve's bed empty.

As George came out of the bedroom Maggie barreled into him and ran out the door.

"Steve, where are you?" she yelled.

She heard Steve scream for her and took off running in that direction. George grabbed her shoulder.

"Maggie stop, you at least need to put shoes on if we are going to make any attempt to find him."

Maggie ran back to the trailer and grabbed her shoes. As she was sliding them on Mike and Katrina as well as Charles & Gloria came out of their trailers.

"What's going on?" Mike yelled.

"Something has taken Steve," Maggie cried.

George told them what had transpired and Charles and Mike ran back into their trailers to grab their guns. As they came back out George told Charles to stay at the camp and protect the rest of the group. George told him to get everyone in the same trailer since they would be easier to keep safe if they were all in a group. Maggie, George, & Mike ran off towards where they last heard Steve screaming. They were shining their flashlights on the ground looking for any sign of Steve or whatever was carrying him away. As they reached the creek Mike looked down and saw a footprint in the soft ground.

"Look at this," Mike said

"What the hell kind of print is that?" George asked.

"I don't know."

"Come on let's follow it, we have to find Steve," Maggie said.

They crossed the river and headed in the direction towards the mountain side hoping they could find Steve before it was too late.

Meanwhile up ahead near the top of the mountain Steve was squirming and trying to get away from the beast that was carrying him. The beast stopped for a minute and Steve took the opportunity to fight as hard as he could. He started kicking and punching at the animal with little effect. The beast lifted Steve up by his arms, looked directly into Steve's eyes and growled. Steve stopped fighting and started to cry and then began screaming for his mom. The beast put Steve under one arm and took off running down the next valley.

"I can hear him screaming for me," Maggie yelled as she started running up the hill.

"Maggie, wait we have to make sure we follow the trail so we don't lose track of where they went," Mike said.

"I'm going up this mountain I hear my son yelling for me up there, I don't give a damn where the trail leads, I'm going straight up the hill."

"Fine, you and George head up the hillside and I will follow the tracks, that way if you don't see him we haven't lost any time."

George and Maggie started running up the mountain side as fast as they could. It took them another fifteen minutes to reach the top. When they got to the top they had to stop to catch their breath.

"STEVE," Maggie yelled, hoping the beast had released her son and she would get a response. They didn't hear a thing and Maggie began to cry. George went over and gave her a hug and while he was doing this he saw something over on the ground near a tree.

"Maggie look."

Maggie turned around and ran over to the spot where George was pointing. There was a sock on the ground.

"George this is Steve's sock he was here. We have to figure out which way they went."

They both began looking at the ground but it was so rocky that it was hard to see any footprints.

George began walking around hoping to see tracks going in a specific direction. As his circle began to get bigger he saw what he thought was a track going down into the next valley.

"Maggie they went this way, come on let's go."

Just as they started down the hillside Mike yelled up to them.

"Guys are you up here?"

"Yes we are. They have headed into the next valley." George replied.

"Ok hold up for one second I'm almost there."

Mike got to the top of the hill and leaned against a rock to catch his breath.

"Alright George & Maggie, we need to send for help, we aren't going to be able to catch up with them."

"We are not giving up, I'm going after my son with or without you guys." Maggie cried.

"Just hear me out Maggie. Let George and myself continue the search, and you go back to the trailers to let everyone know what happened and head out to call for help. This is the best chance we have for finding Steve. We don't know where he was taken and there are only three of us out searching right now. We need more help."

Maggie took a deep breath and shook her head. Even though she didn't want to turn around, she knew this was the best option for finding Steve.

George gave his wife a hug and promised that they wouldn't give up searching for Steve. She turned around and started down the hillside while George and Mike headed into the next ravine.

47

Barry and his team were headed down the trail looking for signs of struggle or any sign of Jim for that matter. They stopped at the spot where Barry & Gabe had seen the blood and foot prints. They then spread out in a line and began to follow the drag marks into the brush. Barry was at the center of the group following the drag marks and it was apparent something big had been drug through the brush. After a few minutes Barry's flashlight hit something reflective up ahead.

"Everybody stop, I see something up ahead." Barry stated.

The team halted as Barry and one of the searchers started walking towards what was laying on the ground. As they got closer Barry could tell it was a body. He looked around to make sure nothing was going to attack him and then ran up to the body. "Shit" he muttered to himself.

"We found him, set up a perimeter." Barry stated.

"Is he alive?" one of the searchers asked.

Based on the glazed over eyes and the pool of blood behind Jim's head it was obvious that Jim was no longer alive.

"No" was the only word that Barry could get out.

Barry bent down and closed Jim's eyes, he then pulled off his own jacket and put it over Jim's face. They had been deputies together for about ten years and Barry knew Jim to be one of the best out there.

"Let's get this area taped off, nothing is to come near Jim. I want two of you to stay here with Jim while we get homicide up here to help with this investigation. We are no longer dealing with only a missing persons case. We now have the murder of a Sheriff's deputy to figure out."

Gabe was waiting for the remaining Search & Rescue members to show up and figured that he would start creating a search grid on a map. He searched Jim's truck and found a map underneath his seat. He had just laid it out on the hood of his truck when he started to hear chatter over the radio.

"Gabe, are you there?"

Gabe could tell something was wrong. Barry was on the other end of the radio and didn't sound like himself. He opened the door to grab his radio that was charging and answered the call.

"Yes I'm here, have you found him?"

"Yes, we found him. He is no longer with us. We need to get homicide up here to help with this investigation."

"Son of a Bitch. I shouldn't have let him head back out of the cave alone," Gabe said.

"We all second guess our decision's afterwards Gabe, but this isn't the time or place to do it."

"Your right Barry, thanks for snapping me out of it, I will call for homicide to head up to the area. Are you guys taping off a perimeter?"

"Yes we are in the process right now, we have taped off around Jim's body and will start taping off the drag locations next. I'm going to leave two searchers here with Jim's body to make sure it isn't disturbed."

"Okay I will see you when you get back to the parking lot."

Gabe radioed up to the helicopter and asked them to relay down to dispatch that they needed to dispatch homicide up to the cave. He didn't want to say whom it was for in case any of Jim's family happened to be listening to the radio at home.

Gabe then turned back to the map and process of creating a search grid. There was nothing more that could be done for Jim so he decided the best thing he could do would be to prepare the search area so they could begin their search for the opening of the cave and hope that they would find Rob and possibly Jake as soon as possible.

Down in Cherryton Terry woke to the chatter on the radio. After hearing that they were sending homicide up to Lakota cave he decided that he had sat around enough and that he was going head up the canyon and help out however he could. He got dressed, and then woke up Joselyn to let her know where he was going. After giving her an update on the situation and giving her a kiss goodbye he headed out the door. He hopped into his patrol car and drove off towards the canyon.

He knew if he went the speed limit it would take him roughly one and a half hours to get to Lakota Cave, so he flipped on his lights and drove as quickly as possible up the winding canyon.

SATURDAY

48

Maggie hiked back down towards the camp as quickly as possible. She knew she needed to get help up here if they were going to have any chance of saving Steve. More than once she almost fell while trying to run down the hill through the brush.

Slow down or you're going to fall and be no help to Steve, she thought to herself.

When she arrived back in camp she yelled out for Charles who came running out of his trailer.

"Did you find him?"

"No, but we found tracks at the top of the hill, George and Mike are going after him. We need to go call for help."

As she was explaining to Charles what they had found she looked over at Charles trailer and saw the scared faces of the other kids looking out the trailer window.

"Katrina and Clara already left to go get help, I know where that canyon comes out. Let's jump on the UTV and see if we can't cut them off. Gloria can stay here and protect the kids, she is a better shot than I am anyway."

Maggie nodded her head in agreement. Charles went over to the trailer and told Gloria what their plan was while Maggie grabbed a jacket out of her trailer. They met over at the UTV and took off towards the outlet of the canyon that George & Mike would be hiking down.

Meanwhile Katrina and Clara were just getting to the highway when they saw a police car race by with its light flashing and headed towards Bear Lake. Katrina flashed her lights to try and get his attention, but it didn't work. She pulled out onto the highway following the police car.

"Aunt Katrina I think we may be going a little fast," Clara stated.

"We have to try and catch up to that officer, it is our best chance to get help."

Katrina pushed on the gas pedal and was finally starting to catch up with the police car. She started flashing her lights again as well as honking and the officer finally pulled over.

Terry saw the truck behind him catching up to him at a high rate of speed and they were flashing their headlights.

I don't have time for this, he thought.

He pulled his car over at the next turn out and the truck pulled in behind him. He climbed out of his car as the driver of the truck exited. "Hold it right there," he said. He pulled out his flashlight and saw a lady standing at the truck door and a teenage girl that looked very frightened sitting in the passenger seat.

Katrina stopped and listened to Terry's orders. Next Terry told Katrina to walk up to him. When she got up to him Terry asked her what was going on and why she flagged him down. Katrina explained the events of what had happened that night as well as all of the strange sightings and what had seemed like innocent events with animals throughout the last two days.

"Ok, I need you to slow down. I am going to repeat back to you what you just said to make sure I understand."

Terry was trying to process everything that Katrina was saying but she was so worked up it was difficult to understand.

After repeating back the story and getting a few corrections Terry seemed to understand the story. Katrina's nephew had been taken from camp during the last few hours. The kids had a few run-ins earlier in the day with animals as well as on Thursday and Katrina was starting to think it may be tied to her nephew being taken. Terry had his doubts about the run ins because during this time of year there was a lot of wildlife on the move as well as cattle roaming the hillsides but after the strange events that had been happening he had to assume that Katrina was telling the truth and either way at the end of the day there was still a young boy that was missing.

"Ok, I have your story straight. I'm going to go up to the top of the canyon and request help be sent to your campground. I will meet you at the Fredericks Basin turn off and we can head to your campsite."

"Ok, thank you!"

Katrina walked back to the truck and as she climbed in, Terry took off up the road to call for more help. Katrina looked over at Clara and could tell she was very worried about her brother.

"Don't worry Clara, he was going to go call for help and would meet us at the turn off. Soon we will have a whole Search and Rescue team up here helping find your brother."

Katrina made a U-turn on the highway and headed back to the Fredericks Basin turn off.

When Terry made it up to the top of the canyon, he grabbed his radio and called down to the Bear Lake dispatch. After relaying the information the dispatch office said they would send a deputy to help coordinate Terry's efforts but unfortunately most of the available deputies were up helping with the search at Lakota Cave.

After getting off of the radio with Bear Lake dispatch he got on his cell phone and called down to the Cherryton Sheriff's Dept. He told them the same story that he had just told the Bear Lake Dispatch and asked for them to send up any available units. The dispatch officer said he would start rounding up available units and transferred the call over to Sheriff Hamilton's phone.

"Hi Sheriff, it is Terry Johnson, I need to see if you can send any help up to Fredericks Basin."

"Jesus Christ what is happening up there. We are spread about as thin as I can imagine with the missing boys and now Deputy Schwartz being killed."

"Was it Jim that was killed?"

"Yes, we aren't sure what killed him, we just know he was attacked while heading out of the cave to call for help. What is going on in Fredericks Basin?"

Terry told him the story about Steve being abducted and how he was hoping that the Sheriff's Dept. could send some help to find him.

"I am almost to the turn off for Lakota cave, when I get there I will send eight Search and Rescue members to Fredericks Basin. Head to the families campground and leave your lights on so they can find you. I'm sure dispatch will send you a few units as well."

"I'm starting to think something big is happening up here Sheriff, I feel like all of these incidents may be related."

"I agree Terry, stay safe and don't let anyone go off on their own. We don't need anyone else getting killed."

Terry hung up his phone and turned his car around and headed back towards Fredericks Basin. When he got to the turn off he saw Katrina and Clara waiting for him. He rolled down his window and told Katrina what had transpired.

"When will they be here? We need to find Steve as quickly as possible."

"It will probably take an hour before we have anyone else up here."

"He will have been gone for three hours by then."

"There isn't much more we can do, the officers and Search & Rescue workers are spread very thin right now. Let's head to your camp and get prepared for the searchers to come."

Katrina started the truck and headed towards camp with Terry following closely behind.

When they arrived back at camp Katrina noticed that the UTV was gone. She ran over to Charles & Gloria's trailer and knocked on the door. Gloria came and peaked out the window to see who it was. Once she realized it was Katrina she opened the door.

"Where is the UTV Katrina asked?"

"Charles & Maggie took it to try and head off whatever had taken Steve. Charles seemed to know where the canyon that the beast had headed down came out."

Katrina introduced Terry to Gloria as well as the kids. Her and Terry went to each trailer and turned on the outdoor lights so they could see what they were doing. They pulled out a map and Katrina marked the spot where Maggie had told Charles & Gloria that she had seen the beast's footprints.

49

As Gabe finished lining out the search grid to look for the opening of the cave the last of the searchers pulled into the parking lot. He called them all over to the hood of the truck and asked one of them to hold up a flashlight so he could go over the search area. He then split the searchers up into three teams of one full time officer and three Search & Rescue staff.

"Alright under no circumstances are you to leave the group. I need you together at all times. I want to find Rob just as bad as the rest of you but I don't need anyone else getting killed. Stick to your groups of four and stay within sight of each other. We are trying to find the opening to the cave that Rob is stuck in. Remember there is someone or something in the cave with him so we need to act quickly and carefully."

Gabe finished showing each search group the area they were going to search as well as handed out a pair of thermal vision goggles to each team. They were going to use them to look for the entry to the cave. Just as the teams were about to head up, the Sheriff pulled into the parking lot.

Sheriff Hamilton opened his door and yelled "hold on for just a few minutes everyone I need to talk to you."

He went over and shook hands with Gabe.

"How are you doing, Sheriff?"

"Well I've been better, I need to split your teams up. I need to send eight members of the Search team back to Fredericks Basin."

"What? That is half of the members."

"I know Gabe but we have a little boy that has gone missing and from the sounds of it the abduction may be tied to Rob's."

Sheriff Hamilton then told the Searchers and Gabe what had happened.

"Damn, this weekend is having a rough start." Gabe said

"Alright everyone we are going to split up the two teams that are staying here are going to break into teams of three with one deputy each. I am going to send out the final two deputies together to search. The eight of you go speak to Sheriff Hamilton about the exact location to meet Terry."

The teams headed out to their search areas hoping to find the entrance to the cave sooner rather than later. As they left the remaining teams headed back to their vehicles so they could drive down to Fredericks Basin.

50

Charles and Maggie drove quickly along the road to the location where Charles believed the canyon ended.

"Around this bend is where the canyon comes out. Let's leave the UTV here and sneak quietly on foot. If they haven't already crossed the road we should be able to stop them."

Maggie nodded her head and they both climbed out of the UTV and headed down the road. Once they could see where the canyon crossed the road they stepped off the side and into the brush.

"Let's wait here and watch for them. If they come across the road I will pull out my gun and try to stop them."

Maggie shook her head in agreement and they both sat in the dark waiting and hoping to see Steve soon.

"Charles, do you think it is possible that they have already crossed the road?"

"No I don't think they could have made it down here that quick. Let's give it a little while and if we haven't seen any movement we will go check."

After thirty minutes or so they were watching the opening in the canyon and they could see flashlights shining on the hillsides.

"Maggie, that has to be George & Mike and they aren't very far away. That means whoever has Steve has to be getting close."

"What if they have already crossed the road and we are wasting time Charles. We have to find Steve soon!"

"I know Maggie, I just don't think someone would have had enough time to get down here and cross the road yet, especially carrying Steve."

Up the canyon Mike and George were moving as quickly as they could trying to catch up to the kidnapper and Steve. They knew they were getting close to the road but were hoping to catch up in case there was a car at the bottom waiting to take Steve away.

"Mike lets go, we have got to be making up time on this prick, there is no way he is going to be able to move quickly carrying Steve."

"Alright, I'm refreshed, let's go."

Mike stood up after getting a drink from the stream and started jogging after George. They had been moving as quickly as they could without losing the kidnappers trail. They figured they had fifteen to twenty minutes until they would be out of the canyon and onto the road.

Back alongside the road Maggie was starting to get anxious.

"Alright Charles we need to go see what is going on Mike & George are making good time but I don't know if they would have caught up to them. They are almost to the road, we need to go see if we can see any tracks."

" I agree Maggie, stay here and I will sneak down this ditch and see if I can see anything without exposing myself to anyone coming out of the canyon."

Charles slowly started crawling down the side of the road staying low enough that no one coming out of the canyon would see him. When he was twenty yards away he looked back at Maggie and started waving for her to come down to him. She crawled as quickly as she could down to Charles.

"What is it Charles did you find something?"

Charles pointed to a branch that had some fabric stuck to it.

"Oh my god that is part of Steve's pajamas."

Maggie put her face in her hands and started crying.

"We are never going to find him are we?"

"Yes we are, we still have a trail to follow and I will be damned if some son of a bitch is going to kidnap my grandson without any repercussions."

Charles stood up to give Maggie a hug just as George and Mike came out of the brush.

"George & Mike, over here."

Charles waved them over to where they were standing and gave them an update on what they had found.

"Has anyone gone for help?" George asked.

"Yes, Katrina and Clara went for help. Hopefully they will be back soon." Charles answered.

"We need to regroup. We can continue to follow this trail but I don't think we are going to catch them without some help."

"I'm not leaving him George, we have to keep searching!" Maggie said, through her sobs.

"We will find our son Maggie. We need to go back to camp and hopefully meet up with whatever help Katrina and Clara were able to find. Once we have done that we can start right back here and continue to track them."

"I'm going to keep searching, you guys can go ahead and go back but I'm not giving up."

"Maggie, no one is giving up. We need to regroup so we can make this search as efficient as possible, it does us no good to be spread out stumbling through the woods." Charles said.

"Dad, why don't you go back with Mike and get the search group together. Maggie & I will keep following this trail so we can hopefully be closer to finding Steve than we are right now."

"I don't think that is a good idea son."

"Dad I understand that it may not be the best idea, but Maggie isn't going to go back and I am not about to leave her out here in the forest by herself."

"Ok George, Mike & I will go back and wait for help to come and then we will come and find you."

They all walked quickly down the road to the UTV. Charles gave George & Maggie a hug and then climbed into his seat along with Mike.

"You two be careful, we will be back as quickly as possible."

"We will Dad, see you soon."

George and Maggie watched the lights from the UTV fade away and then turned around and walked quickly down the road. They were determined to go find their son.

51

Steve had been carried for what seemed like hours. He was too scared to fight against the beast; he was too afraid that he would hurt him. As they were moving through the brush, Steve felt lost & hopeless. On the trek they had traveled up the hillside from the trailer, down a canyon and had crossed the main road. Steve had recognized the road and thought he had heard a UTV coming down the road but unfortunately the beast had quickly gone across the road and headed back into the thick brush. They never stopped moving, continuing alongside the road for a while and then headed up a steep ravine toward the top of another ridge.

When they reached the ridge Steve looked up and could see a helicopter flying north of them with a spotlight shining from it.

Are they looking for me? he thought.

Of course he had no way of knowing that they were looking for another missing boy. The beast carried him down the ridgeline and then headed down a canyon on the opposite side of the ridge from where they had come.

The beast stopped near a small creek and dropped Steve on the ground. The beast bent over and started drinking from the creek.

Steve took advantage of the situation and dove under some bushes and started rolling down the ravine that they were in. The beast turned around, saw him trying to get away and as it charged after him it roared loudly. Steve knew he had to use this chance to get away if possible. He jumped to his feet and started running.

Alex Gonzalez, a deputy with the Sheriff's Dept. was leading one of the search groups looking for Rob. His team was about 1/2 mile away from the parking lot and working around a steep hillside looking for any possible openings to the cave. Alex had the thermal vision binoculars and was looking for openings when he heard a strange roaring sound.

"Did you hear that?" he asked while pulling the binoculars down.

The other members in his search party looked at him and nodded that they had heard the sound.

"It sounded like it came from the next ridge over, let's see if we can work over that way and try to look down the valley. We will probably get a better view of this hillside from over there."

He loaded the binoculars back into his backpack, threw the bag over his shoulder and started hiking. His team got in line behind him and they hiked up to the ridgeline above them. Once they got to the top they followed the ridgeline around the bowl shaped valley. After about twenty minutes they were along the other side and were able to see down into the valley as well as look back at the hillside they were on.

Alex grabbed the thermal vision binoculars out of his backpack. He looked down into the ravine. Down below he could see movement of what looked like a large two legged animal running down the ravine.

"Good god I have been up for too long," he stated."

"What is it?" one of his team members asked.

"Here, take these and look for yourself."

"I don't see anything Alex?"

Alex grabbed the binoculars back and looked down the ravine again. This time he couldn't see anything.

"Before I handed you the binoculars I saw a two legged creature running down the ravine. There was no way it was human because it was moving too quickly through this terrain. I must be going crazy. Here you take the binoculars and keep looking for the cave opening.

52

When Mike and Charles made it back to camp there was a police cruiser sitting in the campsite and everyone was standing around a campfire. Charles felt a sense of relief knowing help was arriving. They climbed out of the UTV and walked over to near the campfire. Charles reached out his hand to Terry and introduced himself.

"I'm relieved that you are here, Officer Johnson. Charles looked around, where is the rest of the calvary?"

"They are on their way. We had an incident with some guys that went missing by Aspen Grove and they seem to have found one of them stuck in Lakota Cave so most of our Search & Rescue team has been routed up there. We have some of the team headed back down the canyon to meet us here so we can continue the search for Steve."

"Glad to hear that, I hope they get here soon. My Grandson has been missing for a few hours."

"Charles, where are Maggie & George?" Gloria asked.

"Maggie wasn't going to give up on finding Steve, so they were still following the tracks that were left."

"I wish they would have come back, we don't need more people missing."

"I know Gloria, I tried to talk them into coming back but Maggie would have none of it so George decided to stay with her."

"Charles and Mike, will you please come over to my car? I have a map that I want to start marking up so we have search grids created when the search team gets here."

The three of them walked over to Terry's patrol car and Terry pulled out a map. Mike showed Terry where they had gone up the mountain and the canyon that they had followed the tracks back down and where George & him met Charles & Maggie. Gloria brought them each a cup of hot coffee and a blueberry muffin.

"Thank you Gloria I prefer doughnuts, it's a cop thing, but this muffin is great!" Terry said.

Meanwhile George and Maggie had been slowly following the tracks of the beast. The tracks went through the thick willows that lined the side of the road and it was tough to see them at times. After roughly a quarter of a mile the tracks seemed to disappear. George and Maggie continued to shine their flashlights in every direction but couldn't seem to see the tracks.

"Where do you think they went?" Maggie asked frantically.

"I don't know, the tracks just seem to disappear."

"They can't just disappear, George. Where did this bastard take my son!"

"Maggie, he is my son as well. I'm trying to do my best to find Steve, your yelling isn't going to help."

Maggie started crying. George walked over and gave her a hug.

"I'm sorry George, I'm just so worried that we aren't going to ever see Steve again."

"I know, but we have to stay calm so we can use our energy to search for Steve. I'm going to walk up this hillside and look around. Maybe I can see something off in the distance, I just don't think they could be very far ahead of us. You stay down here and keep searching for Steve. We need to make sure we can see each other at all times."

George started up the hillside looking for tracks as he went. He could smell the sweet smell of the sage brush as his legs brushed against it. He was hoping he would be able to see further off into the distance once he was up on the hillside. Once he was up to what he thought would be a good lookout point he turned his flashlight off so his eyes could adjust to the dark. After a few minutes George's eyes adjusted and he was impressed how far he could actually see with the moonlight. He could look to the west and see up White canyon as well over the valley to the north and the summit of Wilderness Peak. He kept his eyes peeled for any movement but all was silent. He didn't take much solace in knowing that his son was somewhere out there with a beast that may have decided he was dinner or with some crazed lunatic. He shook those thoughts from his head.

I've got to stay positive. We are going to find him and everything is going to be ok.

"Do you see anything George?" Maggie whispered loudly.

"No, I haven't seen any movement. I think we need to wait here until more help comes, why don't you climb up here and we will keep a lookout.

Maggie started up the hillside and was soon standing next to George. She looked up the hillside and just as she sat down saw something shiny on the ground just a few feet away on the other side of George.

"George, do you see that shiny object on the ground? What is that?"

George got up and walked over to the object and picked the object up.

"It's just a quarter sweetie," he said as he handed the quarter to her.

Maggie sat there for a moment and then her eyes got big.

"I know which way they went."

53

Steve had run roughly one hundred yards down the canyon when he came upon a big grouping of thick brush. He dove into the brush and belly crawled to what he thought was the middle of the brush pile and laid there quietly. Less than a minute later he could hear the beast walking near. Steve didn't move a muscle but it felt like his heart was beating so loudly that there was no way the beast wouldn't hear him. He could hear the beast grunting and sniffing the air and he knew the beast was hunting him. All of a sudden it went silent and Steve couldn't hear anything.

Did it leave? He thought.

Just as that thought crossed his mind a pungent smell came from behind him and he knew immediately that it was the beast.

Steve didn't move; he lay as still as possible hoping it would continue on. He could hear the branches above him moving as the beast tried to find his way through the brush. After a few tense moments everything went silent again.

He moved on, maybe I will get away, Steve thought.

Just as that thought crossed his mind he felt the beast grab his leg and start dragging him through the brush. Steve screamed but that didn't stop the beast as he started up the side of the canyon with Steve's upper body dragging on the ground. Steve tried to keep his head off of the ground as the rocks dug into his shoulders. "Please stop," he cried. The beast continued up the hill. Steve tried to wiggle free, this made the beast even angrier and turned and growled at him and continued up the hill.

Once they were at the top of the canyon the beast turned and looked to the north where Steve could see a helicopter flying around. His only hope was that it would come their way and scare the beast off. As the helicopter continued towards them the beast picked Steve up and carried him along the ridgeline until they came to a group of trees with a sinkhole in the middle of it. The beast threw Steve over its shoulder and started walking into the sinkhole. Once near the bottom Steve could see a small overhang with a hole in it.

This must be his den, I'm done for, he thought.

The beast pushed Steve ahead of him into the small opening and followed him in. Once inside the cave it seemed to open up and looked to have three different corridors. Although it was tough for Steve to tell because the only light was from the moonlight outside. Steve felt the beast grab him under one arm and start carrying him again. He turned so he was looking behind the beast and saw light flickering on the cave wall.

"Is that a fire?" he thought.

The further they got away from the opening the darker it became and soon Steve couldn't see anything around him; it was the darkest place Steve had ever experienced. Eventually the beast threw Steve to the ground and walked away.

Steve didn't know what to do. It was dark and he didn't know where he was. He didn't know which direction to go or how to get out. He started to cry thinking he would never see his family again.

54

Alex and his team had watched as the creature continued lumbering down the canyon as if it was chasing something, it would walk on two feet for a while & then get down on all fours and sniff the ground. The creature then went around a bend in the canyon and they had lost sight of it. They had radioed the helicopter as well as Gabe and reported what they had seen. Gabe told them to try and get eyes on the animal again and asked Tim to finish this portion of his search grid and start heading their way. Tim heard the conversation on the radio & told them they were almost done with the grid square they had been searching and would be there in fifteen minutes.

Alex and his crew started hiking quickly along the ridgeline hoping to get sight on the animal again. They were all tired and their feet were killing them but they all had a feeling that they may have found a lead to where Rob and now Steve may be. They rounded the bend in the ridgeline and stopped to try and see if they could see anything moving in the moonlight. As they all sat looking down into the canyon one of the searchers looked up at the ridgeline across the canyon and thought he saw something move in the trees.

"What is that?"

"What is what?" Alex asked.

"Something is moving over there among those trees at the top of the ridge."

Alex looked up at the ridgeline with the thermal vision binoculars but didn't see anything.

"Are you sure you saw something up there?"

"Yes, I'm sure I saw something up there but I'm not sure if it was the same creature, it seemed big though."

"Let's sit here for a few minutes and wait for the helicopter, they will be able to get a better view and can point us in the right direction. There is no reason to waste our energy."

About ten minutes later they could hear the helicopter coming up behind them.

"Why don't they have their search light on?" asked one of the newer Search and Rescue members.

"They are using thermal vision headsets and the light would obstruct their view." One of the other searchers answered.

"Alex, we should be just about to your location." Tim radioed.

"Yes you are, we are just below the top of the ridge about a quarter of a mile to your left."

Tim turned the helicopter and headed along the ridgeline. Soon he could see the glow from the search crew in his thermal imaging goggles.

"Alright I see you Alex, where do you want me to search?"

"We last saw the animal in the canyon below us, however we saw something move over on the other ridge in the trees that are right on top that we think you should check out."

Tim looked below him into the canyon and didn't see any large animals moving about. He moved the helicopter slowly across the canyon looking for any movement. Once they were over the other ridge he looked around and couldn't see anything of significance.

"Jared, I'm going to slowly fly over this ridge will you open the door and look out over the edge just to make sure we aren't missing anything as we fly over."

Jared strapped his harness on and clipped into the helicopter. He then opened the side door as the wind from the blades started blowing into the helicopter. He leaned out over the edge and put his feet on the skids. Tim slowly started moving the helicopter over the grouping of trees. At first Jared didn't see anything but as they got over the middle of the trees he saw some blue start showing up on his thermal goggles.

"Hey I'm getting some blue on my goggles, we may have found an opening to the cave."

55

"That's Steve's quarter! I gave it to him at the gas station."

George was trying to calm Maggie down and get her to wait for the search crews but she was having none of it, she knew that Steve had been taken up the hillside and wanted to continue their search immediately.

"Come on George we have to head up this hillside, this is the way that Steve went."

"Maggie, how do you know that is Steve's quarter? Maybe someone dropped it while hiking."

Maggie was growing more irritated by the moment.

"I know this is Steve quarter because I gave it to him in the goddamn store! How many quarters have you seen with Yellowstone on it? Better yet how many of them have been painted pink? I know this is the one that I gave Steve!"

George could tell Maggie knew in her heart that this was Steve's quarter and he knew not to disregard her intuition.

"Ok, we will head up the hillside, but I think we need to wait for the rest of the search crew to get here. If we head up the hillside they won't know where we went and we will have no help."

"I'm not waiting, I'm going up there with or without you."

"Maggie, we are going to need help, we can't just continue to chase after them without thinking or we will never find him! We need to wait for help."

Maggie could hear the frustration and worry in George's voice.

"Fine, I will give them thirty minutes."

As they sat there shivering from the cold they could hear a helicopter on the other side of the mountain.

"Maggie, do you hear that maybe that is the help we have been waiting for!"

Back at the campsite Terry & Charles were finishing up the map they were going to use for a search grid when the Search & Rescue team drove up the road. They shined a spotlight over into camp and recognized Terry's squad car so they pulled in.

All of them walked over to stand by the fire as it was getting colder the closer it got to sunrise. Terry briefed them on what had happened and explained where they were going to begin their search.

After assigning the search crews to teams and making sure they understood the general areas where they were going to be looking for Steve they all headed back to their vehicles. Charles & Mike were going to lead them to where they had left Maggie & George. Once they had found where they had already searched they would begin the grid search.

Mike walked over to Katrina and gave her a kiss.

"Go find Steve, be careful but do whatever you have to to make sure he comes back."

"We will sweetie, failure isn't an option. We will see soon. I love you!"

"I love you too."

Mike walked over to Charles' trailer where he was in the same conversation with Gloria.

"Ready Dad?"

"Yep, let's go find Steve."

"You guys, be careful out there and bring my Grandson home safely." Gloria said as they were walking over to George's UTV.

They climbed into the UTV, Charles turned it on and backed out of the camp spot. He slowly started down the road headed towards where they had left George & Maggie. After a fifteen minute drive they were to the spot where they had last seen them.

"Alright let's see where they went."

They climbed out of the UTV and waited for the rest of the crew to climb out of their vehicles. Once they were circled up Charles showed them what direction Maggie & George had gone.

"Did you hear that Maggie? That sounded like vehicles coming down the road. I bet Dad & Mike are headed back our way. Once we see them I will start flickering the flashlight so that they see us."

"Look over there, I can see the prints from George & Maggie's boots headed through the brush along the road."

He walked over to the prints.

"It looks like they headed the same direction as the road. Dad, why don't you take the UTV and go up the road and see if you can see them."

"I will go with you Charles. Why don't one of you go with Mike to follow the trail in case we don't see them from the road and the rest of you wait here. We will radio you if we see them" Terry stated.

Charles and Terry climbed into the UTV and headed down the road.

"Look Maggie there are headlights coming down the road. It looks like it is a UTV."

George started flickering his flashlight at the road trying to get their attention.

"Charles stop the UTV, I bet that is your son. I can see a flickering light up on the side hill."

George and Maggie saw the UTV stop and headed down the hillside. When they got to the bottom they saw it was Charles, but he had someone else with him. Charles & Terry climbed out of the UTV and walked over to the side of the road. George stuck out his hand

and introduced himself. Terry shook George & Maggie's hands and told them what the search plan was.

Maggie interjected "Thank you for planning this out, but we need to head up that hillside. I know that is where my son is."

She then told Terry and Charles about losing the trail over in the brush and how they had found the quarter on the hillside. Terry had his doubts but Maggie was very insistent that they needed to search up that way.

"Ok, let me call the search crews up here and we will redirect one of the search crews up the hillside. I think it would be a bad idea to send everyone up there until we find more evidence."

They could now hear the helicopter over the ridge again.

"Is that helicopter coming to help us?" Maggie asked Terry.

"Not at the moment, it is on another search currently."

Terry then told them about Rob & Jake missing but left out the fact that Jim had been killed. There was already enough worry and he didn't want to send the parents over the deep end.

Terry called the search crew to come down the road and meet them. Once they arrived a few minutes later Terry explained the situation and decided they would have one search crew continue in the brush along the road, one search crew would head across the road to look for any signs and the remainder of the team would go up the hillside.

The teams split up to start their searches. Maggie, George & Mike were going to head up the hillside with that search team. Charles & Terry were going to stay along the road and direct the search teams while the two other teams would search in the directions that they were given.

56

Steve had calmed down after crying for a while. He knew he had to find a way out of this cave if he was going to be found. He slowly started crawling hoping to find a way out. He didn't know which direction to head but he knew he needed to start moving. He had only crawled a few feet when he felt a wall in front of him. He then made the decision that he would turn to his left and start following the wall.

After crawling for a while he stopped to take a break. He sat in the quiet wondering if he had made the right decision and wishing he was back in the trailer with his family. Suddenly he heard some movement in the dark.

"Hello?"

Steve heard something making a groaning sound and wasn't sure if he was scared or relieved. He started crawling towards the sound and eventually felt something soft. He realized it was a leg and once he touched it the owner of the leg started groaning even louder, the person was shivering from the cold.

"You have to be quiet or the beast will come back" Steve said.

He started shaking the person trying to wake them up and eventually the person started to become coherent.

"Ow my head" The voice said.

"Did the beast bring you here? My name is Steve."

"What is your name?"

The person still wasn't fully awake and just moaned in pain.

"Where am I?" the person said.

"We are stuck in a cave."

Steve again asked the person their name.

"My name is Rob. Help me I'm freezing."

"I know, we have to find a way out of here." Steve said.

He had even more determination to find a way out now that he wasn't on his own. He helped Rob sit up against the wall. This made Rob moan in pain. They sat there for a few minutes waiting for Rob's headache to subside.

Once his head began to clear Rob started to remember what had happened to him.

"If we are going to try to escape we are going to have to stay quiet."

"No kidding, that is what I was just telling you!" Steve replied.

Rob then told Steve about how he had found a hole in the cave and had talked to a Forest Ranger in Lakota cave and how the beast had found him and drug him to another spot in the cave. Steve questioned whether Rob had dreamed this after hitting his head but Rob's story was very persuasive so he decided to believe him. Steve helped Rob to his knees and they began to slowly crawl in a direction that they hoped would lead them to the opening of the cave.

57

Tim & Alex had decided that Tim would try and land the helicopter on the ridge so that Jared could jump out and examine the possible cave opening while Alex and his team back tracked and worked their way to the opening. It would take Alex and his team roughly an hour to hike around to the other side given the terrain, but if Jared was able to get onto the ground and verify the opening they could call for backup and get more searchers headed in that direction. Tim circled the helicopter a few times trying to find the perfect spot to touch down, unfortunately the ridge was too narrow and he didn't know if he would be able to land.

"Jared it doesn't look like there is a spot flat enough for me to land on. I can hover just a few feet above the ground if you're willing to jump, but you won't be able to get back on board."

"Tim, can you hear me?"

"Yes Gabe, I hear you."

"I do not want Jared getting off of the helicopter by himself, we have already lost one deputy tonight."

"I understand Gabe but if we don't have him get off and check we may be wasting a lot of time by waiting for Alex and his crew to hike around to this location."

"I don't care, I repeat do not have Jared get off of the helicopter."

"Ok Gabe, you are in command. Let me send you my coordinates so you know where Alex and his team are headed."

Tim read his coordinates off to Gabe and turned the helicopter around.

"Hey Tim, I need you to go and get some information for me. As you know Officer Terry Johnson is down in Fredericks Basin looking for a boy that was taken from his campsite, I'm not sure where they are but we need to get as much information from him as possible to see if these cases are linked. I believe the quickest way to coordinate efforts will be to find out as much information as possible from the boy's family and to either rule out that the cases are tied together or to coordinate both search efforts."

"Affirmative Gabe, we will head that way now."

Tim flew the helicopter in the direction of Fredericks Basin which was only two miles from their current location.

"Hey Tim, how are we going to know where exactly Terry is?"

"Not a clue Jared, I guess we will fly into the valley and look for a patrol car or flashlights"

Alex and his team started their hike, they would be back tracking and headed towards Lakota peak. Nobody had said anything but they all had a bad feeling that Steve's disappearance and Rob's were tied together somehow and they wondered what they would find when they got to the location.

Tim's five minute flight took them over another mountain top and opened into a large valley that was considered the middle of Fredericks Basin, to the south and to the north the canyon walls narrowed. Tim turned to the south and began his descent lower into the canyon, he was planning on flying at an altitude of 150 ft, this way they could make out vehicles and people easier. As they continued to fly they saw vehicle lights on the road.

Terry and Charles were just getting ready to take off down the road in the UTV when a helicopter flew above them and started to hover. Terry assumed it was the Sheriff's department's helicopter; he grabbed his radio to try and make contact.

"This is Officer Terry Johnson with the Cherryton Police dept. Do you read?"

"Roger, I read you. This is Deputy Tim Morrison. Gabe requested I come and get some information from you. Have you talked to the family?"

"Yes I have. The boy's Grandpa is here with me and the parents and uncle are headed up that hillside."

Tim looked to his right and up the mountain about two hundred feet and could see three people on the hillside. He could barely make out their shapes in the moonlight.

"Ok Terry what information can you give me so I can relay it to Gabe?"

Terry explained the situation to Tim and told him what direction they believed the boy had been taken.

"Ok thanks Terry. I will get this information over to Gabe. Round up all of your searchers and I will be back in 15-20 minutes."

"Okay, I will get everyone rounded up so we can decide on how we want to move forward with the search."

Tim proceeded to turn the helicopter around and head towards Lakota Cave. Terry sent a message over the radio to the other searchers.

"Everyone please come back to our original meeting place on the road. We have more information that needs to be passed along so we can decide how to move forward."

George, Maggie and Mike were up on the hillside debating what to do. They didn't want to hike back down the mountain.

"I'm not wasting my time and going back down, George."

"I know Maggie. Let me radio Terry and tell him we will hold tight but we don't want to back track halfway down the mountain side."

George radioed Terry and told him they would hold tight but they weren't coming down the mountain side.

"Roger that George. I will update you as soon as Tim is back and give me more information."

Terry could see the searchers trucks coming back down the road towards him. He got out of the UTV and walked over into the grass trying to find a flat spot for the helicopter to land. He found a spot and started walking around to verify that the helicopter wouldn't hit any rocks as it came in for a landing.

After that all they could do was wait for Tim to get back.

Meanwhile Tim was bringing the helicopter down for a landing in the Lakota Cave parking lot. As he touched down and shut the helicopter off Gabe climbed out of his truck and started walking towards him.

The rotors stopped and Tim & Jared climbed out of the helicopter.

"How are things going Gabe?"

"We are just waiting for the detectives & coroner to come up and get Jim's body, they should be here any minute. Alex and his team are still working their way around the hillside towards the opening. What information did you get from Terry?"

Tim told Gabe about what had happened with the boy that was missing.

"Gabe, I think that these cases may be related. The direction that the tracks are heading are right towards where we are searching for Rob."

Gabe sat there thinking for a minute.

"Do you think that whatever Alex saw was the beast carrying Steve?"

"I guess it's possible. Based on the rough timelines we have been given they would match up. It is just hard to believe."

"Alright Tim head back to Terry and give him this satellite phone. We need to be in direct contact. I want you to tell Terry that we think these cases are related and explain to him what Alex saw."

Tim and Jared headed back to the helicopter. They climbed in and Tim started the helicopter and slowly began his climb out of the parking lot. Just as they were getting ready to start towards Fredericks Basin Jared looked out the window he could see the sky was turning a light purple, the sun would be up soon. He then looked down and could see three vehicles pulling into the parking lot. Jared could only assume that it was the detectives and the coroner coming to investigate Jim's death. Tim pointed the helicopter in a southwest direction and headed towards Fredericks Basin.

58

"Look!" Steve whispered. Up ahead Rob noticed the faint light as well.

"Maybe that is the way out," Steve said excitedly.

"Calm down Steve, we need to stay quiet. We don't know where the beast is."

They slowly crawled further down the cave. They could see the light getting brighter.

"Stop here for a second Steve. I'm getting dizzy."

Rob could feel his head beginning to spin. They both stopped and sat against the wall. Rob started to feel like he was going to pass out.

"Steve, I need to lay down. My head is killing me. I think we need to wait here for a few minutes."

"Ok you wait here and I will crawl up further and see if I can find the cave opening."

"No wait here with me please I don't want the beast to catch you sneaking out."

He said that wanting to sound like he was protecting Steve, but deep down he didn't want to be left alone.

"Ok we will wait here for a little bit."

They sat there quietly for a few minutes when Steve began to hear Rob breathing deeply and then his breathing began to slow.

"Rob?"

There was no answer. He shook Rob to make sure he was ok but he didn't respond. Steve sat there for a few more minutes and shook Rob again, still no response.

I need to go get help, Steve thought.

"I will be back, Rob. I'm going to go get help."

Steve started to slowly crawl along the wall towards the light hoping that he would find the opening.

He crawled and soon could see the light that they were seeing was flickering.

Is that a fire? he thought.

Steve began to slowly crawl towards the light. He crawled for another few minutes trying to move very slowly and quietly.

I have to be getting close to the opening that has to be the same flickering light I saw when I was brought into this place.

He slowly continued to crawl but stopped suddenly when he heard a growl to his left. He sat quietly waiting to be grabbed by the beast. He waited in darkness and silence for a few minutes but the beast never came. Steve started to crawl again, getting closer and closer to the opening. He could now see the faint light from the moonlight outside. He wanted to run as fast as he could but knew that would be a mistake so he continued his slow crawl.

The opening started to get bigger as Steve got closer. He could also see that the flickering light was down a different corridor.

"How could there be a fire in this cave if there is no smoke?" he thought.

He was tempted to go investigate where the light was coming from, but was afraid of what he might find. He sat in the dark getting ready to make the last push to get out of the cave opening when he suddenly heard voices coming from the direction of the flickering light.

59

"We need to get out of here. This isn't what we had planned." Jake said loudly.

Bill, Jake's dad, put his hand on his son's shoulder.

"Calm down son, we need to adapt to the circumstances. I know we didn't plan on things going like this but panicking isn't going to fix it."

"Calm down? There are helicopters flying around above us! You said they wouldn't find us up here. How would they know to search here?"

"They haven't found us yet. We just need to lay low and keep quiet for a few days. Once this story is out we will have the hills to ourselves and our cattle will be able to free range the entire area without people harassing them."

"Dad, you promised me Rob would be fine and now one of those god damn beasts has beat the shit out of him. You saw how badly he was hurt when he was first brought in. Bill sat there thinking for a minute and then smiled.

"Son, you're a genius! What we need to do is go find Rob and the boy, once we have done that we can help them out of this cave. That will be our alibi, we were able to find them and we were assisting with their rescue!"

"That is a great plan dad, but remember I'm supposed to be missing as well also what about when they come into the caves to search for the beasts?" They will find our camping equipment as well as the beast's lair.

"We will stow our equipment away deep in the tunnel, further than where we found Rob. They will want to know where we found Rob so we will show them but we won't take them down any of the other branches of the cave. We will come back in a couple of weeks and remove our equipment and there won't be anybody that knew we were here."

"What about the fact that I'm supposed to be missing as well?"

"We will tell the police that you were scared for your life when you were chased by the beast. You hiked down to the highway and hitchhiked with a trucker back home. That is when we decide to go look for Rob."

"I don't know dad, I'm having a hard time thinking that they are going to believe this story."

"We will just have to stick with it. We are the only two that know that truth so they won't have a choice but to believe us. Now grab our flashlights let's go see where Rob and the little boy are at."

60

Steve debated whether he should hurry and get out of the cave or if he should sneak closer to the voices and hear what they were talking about.

His curiosity got the best of him and he slowly crawled to where he could hear the voices better.

He heard Jake & Bill discuss their plans and he knew he would need to get out of the cave before they saw him. If he was caught here in the cave he would have ruined their plans and he was sure that they would kill him.

After hearing Jake's dad tell him to grab their flashlights so they could go search, Steve decided he needed to make a run for it. He moved as quickly and quietly as he possibly could toward the entrance of the cave.

Once he was there he climbed his way out of the narrow opening and noticed it was still dark outside. He climbed as quickly as he could and made his way to the top of the sinkhole. Far to the east he could see the sky was turning a purple color as the sun came up. He took off running down the ridge line and into some trees hoping he could hide here for a few minutes to make sure nothing was following him and then he would go find help.

Meanwhile back in the cave Jake had just grabbed their flashlights when they had heard something moving from another portion of the cave. They both looked at each other and immediately ran towards the opening. As they rounded the corner they could hear something scurrying out of the cave.

"What do you think that was Dad?"

"I'm not sure. It must have been some sort of animal."

"You don't think it was Rob do you?"

"No way he would have made more noise and I think that nosey little brat that was taken will be too busy pissing his pants to find his way out of the cave. He will be too worried about one of those beasts catching him again. Now come on we need to go save Rob before anyone finds the entrance and we don't get the chance to be heroes."

Jake & Bill continued their way to the entrance. Once they were there Jake went to shine his flashlight outside but Bill immediately grabbed his arm.

"Son, are you trying to get us caught? If you shine that light outside, someone might see it."

Jake shook his head. "Sorry I didn't think about that."

They walked down the left chamber of the cave and passed the arm of the cave where the beasts had their den and followed the tunnel figuring that the beast would have dropped Rob & the boy half way down the tunnel like they had trained them. If this was correct they would find them in roughly ½ of a mile. They continued down the cave chamber and after only another few minutes they saw Rob laying on the ground and immediately knew something was wrong. "Shouldn't he be farther down in the cave Dad?"

"Yes we have trained these damn animals to take their catch further back in the tunnel, he must have crawled back."

"Where is the boy? Do you think he is still farther back in the tunnel?"

"Yes, probably. Come on, let's go see if we can wake Rob up, maybe he knows where the boy is."

They walked over to Rob and noticed he looked even worse than before.

"Dad, he doesn't look good. What the hell happened to him?"

"I don't know son, he must have tried to fight against the beasts. Just remember when we wake him up we have to stick to our story."

Jake bent down and shook Rob's shoulder.

"Rob wake up, Rob are you ok."

Rob started to stir a little bit and eventually opened his eyes.

"Jake is that you? I thought you were dead. We have to get out of here before that animal finds us."

Rob tried to sit up but his head started spinning so he leaned against the wall. He looked over at Jake and noticed another man standing with him.

"Who is that?"

"It's my Dad. Don't you recognize him?"

"Don't worry Rob we are going to get you out of here," Bill said.

"Where is Steve, did he find you?"

"Who is Steve?" Bill asked.

"He was a little boy that had been taken by the beast. He was here in the cave with me. We were trying to find our way out when I started to get dizzy and needed to lay down. I told him to stay here with me but he must have decided to go for help.

Jake & Bill both looked at each other, they immediately knew what they had heard climbing out of the cave, or better yet who they had heard. Now all they could do is take Rob out of the tunnel and pretend they didn't know about the boy.

61

Tim & Jared arrived back in Fredericks Basin with the satellite radio just as Maggie & George were finding their way back down the mountain. They had decided that it would be better to have all the information possible before they started climbing again. He shut down the helicopter and climbed out along with Jared as Terry was walking over in his direction.

"Do you have any more information Tim?"

"Yeah we do, Gabe wants you to call him on this satellite phone to discuss how to move forward."

Tim handed the phone over to Terry.

Terry started to dial the number Gabe had written down as George and Maggie walked over.

"What is going on, why aren't we looking for Steve?" Maggie said.

"Maggie, George, this is Tim and Jared, they are with the Sheriff's dept. They have been working on the search for the boy that I told you was missing. We are going to coordinate this search with that team since your son had been taken in the direction of their search."

"Ok let's get started, why are we wasting time?"

"I need to call Gabe and get the search coordinated so we all can work together efficiently. Give me a few minutes and I will know more."

"Honey, let's go talk to my dad and brother for a minute and let Terry make the call to the other officer."

George wrapped his arm around her shoulder and they walked towards the UTV where Mike & Charles were sitting.

"How are you guys holding up?" Mike asked.

"I would be better if they would hurry up with this search. They are taking their sweet time while my son's chances of being found continue to dwindle," George said.

Meanwhile Terry looked down at the number again and dialed it. After a few rings Gabe picked up.

"Terry, good to hear from you how are things on that end of the search?"

"We are trying to get coordinated so we can begin our search, but I thought I would call you first. Tim said you had some information for me?"

"Yes I do. After speaking with Tim and Alex we believe we may have spotted the boy that is missing from over in Fredericks Basin. To make a long story short, Alex and his search team saw some type of two legged creature carrying something that would match the size description of Steve. They lost sight of it for a while and then one of the searchers saw movement on a ridge across from where they were sitting. Tim flew his helicopter over the location and they saw a possible opening to a cave but no sightings of the little boy."

"Wait a two legged creature, so you think this is a kidnapping?"

"Well currently we aren't sure what is happening."

"Ok so what do you think our plan of attack should be Gabe?"

"Why don't you guys keep searching up the Basin for Steve and we can have Tim continue to fly a grid between your location and ours. The sun is going to be up in about an hour and that will help the search for Steve, but hinder the search for finding the cave opening."

"Sounds like a plan Gabe, I will let our search team know the plan and continue to search the valley."

Terry hung up the phone and sighed. He knew this wasn't going to go over well with Steve's parents.

62

Alex and his team moved deliberately across the hillside. They had now back tracked from where they had started, scrambled down a cliffside and were making their way across the ridge towards the possible cave entrance.

"That sunrise sure is a beautiful sight," one of the searchers commented.

The sky had transitioned from a dark purple to a lighter shade and now was on its way to a rose colored sky.

"Let's get moving. We only have about a quarter of a mile until we get to the group of trees where they believe the cave entrance is." Alex said.

While the sky was beautiful, they were also thankful that the day would soon be here which would mean an easier search as well as some warmth.

Steve had been hiding in the bushes for what seemed like forever and was trying to decide what to do. He knew that he needed to get moving if he was going to get away from the people in the cave, but he also didn't want to get caught out in the open by one of their crazed beasts. The sky was continuing to get lighter as the day wore on. Finally he decided it was time to move and slowly climbed out from behind the brush. He looked down the ridge and was getting ready to head back towards camp when he saw people coming down the ridgeline in the opposite direction. He thought they were coming from Lakota cave but couldn't be sure. If he would have waited for another couple of minutes he would have missed them because they would have been behind the grouping of trees where the cave entrance was.

Do I run to them? What if they are working with the people in the cave? he thought.

He decided that he would climb back into the brush and stay where he was at for a while and see if he could tell whom they were with before he headed in their direction.

As the hikers got closer to him Steve could see that one of them had a Sheriff's jacket on. Steve decided he would take a chance and hope that the guy was actually a Sheriff's deputy. Now his only risk would be sneaking back by the cave entrance without getting caught. Steve slowly climbed out of the brush and hiked quietly towards the cave entrance. He decided he would work his way down into the ravine and stay away from the cave entrance. After he made his way around the trees he climbed back towards the top of the ridge and stopped in a small grouping of shrubs so he could catch his breath. After a few minutes he peeked his head out of the shrubs and could see the hikers were only about one hundred yards away. Steve got a rush of energy and ran out of the bushes and towards the hikers.

"Look" one of the searchers said. Alex looked up and could see a young boy running in their direction. They all stopped as the boy ran towards them. When the boy got close he stopped.

"Are you guys the good guys?" Steve cried out.

"Yes, we are with the Sheriff's Dept. Are you Steve?"

"Yes" Steve said as he crumpled to his knees and started crying. Alex walked up to him.

"Come on son, you are safe now. Let's get you home."

"NO ,you can't. There is another boy in the cave named Rob."

"Is he alive?" Alex asked

"Yes... Well he was when I left him. He had some injuries and passed out. He asked me to stay with him but I wanted to get help so I left."

The searchers all looked at each other relieved. Soon this long ordeal would be over.

"Ok we will go help him. We need to get you back to your parents. I'm going to have you go with these two guys. Their names are James & Derek and they are search and rescue members who will take you back to Lakota cave and we will get you back to your parents as soon as we can."

"Make sure you help Rob."

"We will now go ahead and eat this candy bar and then James and Derek will hike back with you."

"Wait there are two other people that are down there as well. I think they are bad. One was upset about how Rob wasn't supposed to get hurt in their plan. The other said they would pretend they were there to help him and they would be heroes. I think they might have been the ones that kidnapped us."

"Was it a person or an animal that kidnapped you?"

"It was some sort of huge creature but I think they somehow were controlling them."

Alex looked incredulously at Steve.

"I know it sounds crazy but I think that is what happened, I'm not lying."

"I believe you, James & Derek will get you to safety and I promise we will get to Rob."

Steve, James, & Derek began their long trek back to the Lakota Cave parking lot.

Alex pulled out his radio.

"Gabe do you read?"

"Roger, I can hear you."

"Well I have some good news & bad news. We have found Steve. He is in good shape James & Derek are going to walk him back to base camp. Also the spot Jared thought was a cave opening is actually a cave opening and from what Steve has told us Rob is down there. From the sounds of it he is injured pretty badly. We are going to need you to send a gurney and some reinforcements to help get him out."

"That is great news! I will get help headed your way. Now what is the bad news?"

"Steve said Rob is not the only one in the cave and based on the conversation that he heard he thinks they may be the ones behind this kidnapping."

"Ok, well I want you guys to play it safe, get to a location where you can keep an eye on the cave opening and I will send as many reinforcements as possible.

Gabe radioed the other crews and called them back. He asked the four search & rescue members that had just arrived to grab a gurney out of the ambulance on site and head towards the cave location; two of the EMT's volunteered to go as well while the other two stayed back. They wanted to make sure they had help here at the parking lot in case a search member came back injured. He also requested that three of the Sheriff's deputies that were maintaining the perimeter around Jim to grab their rifles and go to the site. They all grabbed their equipment and headed out. It would take them roughly an hour to get to the location. After everyone had left Gabe grabbed the satellite phone and dialed the number of the phone Terry was carrying.

63

Terry was explaining the situation and the plan to everyone that was in his search group as well as Steve's family.

"We are not going to wait and waste time searching for Steve in this canyon when I KNOW for a fact that he was taken up that hillside." Maggie shouted.

"What if you are wrong and he wasn't taken that way? There are plenty of people searching just a few miles over for both of these missing kids. Tim & Jared are going to fly a planned search grid and see if they can see anything from above. Our directions were to search this canyon to make sure we can rule it out."

"I'm not wrong I know that is the direction he was taken!"

"Ok, well you and your family are more than welcome to continue your own search if you would like. The rest of us were given instructions to search this canyon so that is what we are going to do."

Just then the satellite phone began to ring. Terry walked over to his backpack and grabbed the phone.

"This is Officer Johnson."

"Terry, it is Gabe. I have some good news for you. We have found Steve and he is fine, he has a few bumps and bruises but mainly he is just scared. Two of the team members are on their way back with him to Lakota Cave."

"That is great news!"

"Well hold up before you get too excited. Steve had been taken to a cave and was stuck in there with Rob. From what Steve said Rob was in bad shape."

"Any word on Jake? Was he there as well?"

"Steve didn't say anything about another victim being in there. He did however state that there were two people that were in the cave and one of them was upset that Rob had been injured. We have reason to believe that they may be involved with the kidnapping."

"Wait, so it wasn't an animal that kidnapped them?"

"Currently we are unsure exactly how this has played out. We have deputies and EMT's on their way to the cave opening. I just wanted to let you know as soon as possible so you could tell Steve's family members."

"Thanks for the information Gabe, I really appreciate it. I was about to have a mutiny on my hands. Stay safe."

Terry hung up the phone and smiled at Maggie.

"Well I have some good news. Steve has been found. He is scared but safe."

"Where is he at? I need to see him right now."

"He is being taken to the Lakota Cave parking lot. You were correct that he was taken towards the east and didn't stay in the canyon."

"Come on let's go George we need to get to our truck so we can get up there."

"Hold on Maggie, I'm going to have Tim & Jared fly you & George over to the Lakota cave parking lot. There will be an ambulance there that can check Steve out when he gets back and you guys can meet up with him."

"Thank you. I'm sorry I have been so abrasive I'm just worried about my son."

"No apologies needed, I can't imagine what you have gone through. As for the rest of us, let's head back to the Jacobs campsite and regroup."

Tim, Jared, Maggie, & George climbed up into the helicopter and started their short flight over to Lakota Cave.

After the sound from the helicopter diminished one of the searchers asked Terry, "what about the other two boys that are missing? Have they been found?"

Terry relayed the story about Rob and said there was no word on Jake.

"We are going to head back to the Jacobs camp and regroup. Gabe is quite busy right now so maybe we can get a little rest while we wait to hear how we are going to proceed."

They all climbed back into their vehicles and headed back to the camp. When they pulled up Gloria and Katrina were sitting by the fire. When Clara looked out the window and saw the caravan pull up she jumped out of bed, grabbed her shoes and headed out the door. A little earlier her Grandma had ordered her to bed to get some sleep, but she was unable to under the circumstances.

As Mike and Charles pulled up Gloria and Katrina stood up and started walking over to them. Clara swung the door open "Grandpa, where are my parents?"

They all walked over to the fire and Mike relayed the information about Steve as Terry and the rest of his crew sat down on the ground to get some rest. He had intentionally left out the information about Rob and the possible suspects as he didn't want to worry his mom, wife or niece.

"What great news, I'm so glad Steve is ok, come on Clara and Katrina let's go make these guys some breakfast."

"It's ok ma'am you don't need to cook for us." Terry said.

"Oh I insist, you guys helped find our grandson alive and deserve some good food after what you have been through searching for the other boy."

"Alright you twisted my arm." Terry said smiling.

"I want to go see my brother."

"Clara, they will bring him down here as soon as they can. We just need to be patient and let the Officers do their jobs."

64

As Tim flew the helicopter back towards Lakota Cave he intentionally flew out and around the search area. He didn't want to alarm the kidnappers by flying over the area again. The kidnappers had to know that the area was being searched based on all of the activity the night before but he wanted them to think the searchers had moved on.

As the helicopter touched down Maggie was hoping to see Steve already in the parking lot.

Maybe he is in the ambulance, she thought to herself.

Tim touched the helicopter down and went through his shutdown procedures. They all climbed out and started walking over towards Gabe.

"Hi I'm Game Warden Gabe Campbell. Steve is on his way back to us right now and should be here within the hour."

"Thank you so much for your guys' help in finding him. My wife & I are very thankful."

"Yes thank you so much and thank you for the helicopter ride over here, I am glad we will be here when our son gets back."

"I'm going to have you guys go over into the ticket booth and wait for Steve to return, we still have an active investigation into the death of one of our officers as well as trying to find out what is behind your son getting taken."

George & Maggie walked over to the ticket booth and sat down. They were exhausted but grateful that Steve was safe and they were hoping that the other missing people would be brought back safe as well.

On the other side of Lakota Peak, the Sheriff's deputies and EMT's passed Steve, Derek, & James on their way back to the parking lot. They stopped for a few minutes to check Steve out since they wouldn't be at the parking lot when they got there. Other than the few scrapes & bruises from being attacked by the beast Steve was fine.

"You got away, pretty lucky kid," one of the EMT's said.

"Please go help Rob, he is in bad shape and I had to leave him in the cave."

"We will do our best, once the Sheriff's Dept. gives us the green light we will go in to help Rob as quickly as possible."

The two groups went their separate ways. Steve and his group headed towards safety and the Sheriff's deputies and EMT's headed toward what they hoped would be a successful rescue and peaceful outcome to this crazy situation.

Alex and his team still had the sinkhole under surveillance. They had initially walked over the sinkhole's edge and could see an opening at the very bottom of the sinkhole. It was roughly the size of a car door and would be hard for anyone who didn't happen to stumble onto it to even know it was there. They knew there were at least three people in the cave, two of which could be armed and dangerous. They could only sit and wait for the Sheriff's deputies to get to the location to decide what to do next.

As the sun came up it gave off a comforting warmth to the team and Alex started dozing off after the long night. Suddenly they heard something coming from the cave entrance. They all froze and waited quietly to see what the noise was. Soon they heard two voices and then they could see two people coming out of the tunnel, one of them they recognized as Rob who was being helped by another young man.

Once they were out of the tunnel another person followed. This one had a semi-automatic rifle and was following the two in front. Alex yelled out to them, "Stop right there and let me see your hands."

"We need help, my friend is hurt." Jake yelled out.

"What are you guys doing, who are you?"

"This is Rob, he is hurt and needs help. I'm Jake Appleton, Rob's friend. We found him in this cave after following one of those beasts to the location."

"Ok, let us help you."

Alex & his team worked their way down into the sinkhole.

"Let's sit Rob down for a minute so we can evaluate him. I'm Deputy Gonzalez with the Sheriff's dept. We have been trying to find Rob all night. I'm glad you guys were able to find him."

Alex knew that these two were possibly behind the kidnappings but since currently he didn't have any other deputies to help back him up he decided to play along with their story and not push it too much just yet.

"Rob, are you feeling ok?"

"My head is killing me and the sun is so bright, I think I'm going to throw up."

At that moment Rob turned to his side and started throwing up. Alex assumed that Rob had a head injury. Once he was done Alex directed the team to get Rob up and into the shade, he also put his sunglasses on Rob to help with the bright sun.

"Alex then turned to Bill. Can I ask your name sir?"

"I'm Bill Appleton, Jake's dad."

"Well Bill I'm certainly glad you were able to find Rob, we were starting to lose hope. I'm going to go Radio the search headquarters and let them know he is safe."

"I'm glad we were able to find him as well. When Jake got home and told us Rob was missing we were very concerned."

"I will be right back Bill, I'm going to go make this radio call."

Bill couldn't tell if Alex believed him or not. He & Jake would have to stick to his story and hope for the best.

Alex walked away out of the trees. He looked down the ridge and could see that there were people headed his way, but it would be another fifteen minutes or so before they got to his location.

He radioed Gabe on the main channel hoping that the deputies that were headed his direction would hear and know what they were walking into.

"Gabe do you read?"

"Yes I hear you Alex. Do you have any updates for us?"

"Yes Rob is out of the cave, there were two people that helped him get out. Their names are Bill & Jake Appleton."

Gabe looked over at Sheriff Hamilton.

"Jake Appleton, that is Rob's friend that was missing."

"You're right Gabe, let's just play it safe. Ask if Jake is ok since we know he was missing as well and leave it at that. Once the other deputies arrive they can all assess the situation and figure out how to handle it."

"Alex glad to hear that Rob has been found, just to confirm Jake Appleton is with him and safe as well?"

"Roger, that is correct. Rob is in pretty bad shape though, we are going to need to wait for the gurney before we can get him out."

"Glad to hear they are both safe Alex, we will see you soon. Be careful out there, we still don't know what these creatures were that attacked them."

Just as Alex finished his radio transmission Bill came walking over to him.

"Everything all right?"

"Yes Bill, everything is good. I was talking to the game warden & the Sheriff and they were relieved to hear that Jake was alright too."

"When Jake got home yesterday and told us that they had both been attacked and how he was able to get away but he wasn't sure what happened to Rob I felt like we needed to get up here and find him. We spend a lot of time hiking & hunting up here so we know the area pretty well."

"I'm glad you were able to find him as well. How did Jake get home yesterday?"

"He said he ran away from the creature that attacked him when it went after Rob and he was able to get to the road and hitchhike with a truck driver."

"Well I'm just glad that we didn't lose anyone else, now we just have to find the creature that took these kids and killed our deputy and neutralize it."

"There was a deputy killed?

"Yes last night one of our deputies that was working the case was killed over by the Lakota Cave parking lot."

The color ran from Bill's face.

"Are you ok Bill?"

"Yes, that is too bad about the deputy, hopefully we can find these monsters and get rid of them."

Bill then walked away and went and sat down and leaned against the trunk of a tree.

65

Once the EMT's and Sheriff's deputies arrived the EMT's evaluated Rob. He had multiple cuts on him as well as possibly broken ribs, but his most concerning injury was his head injury. He had a massive cut on top of his head and they were concerned about him going in and out of consciousness.

They looked at Alex "We need to get him to a hospital as soon as possible, do you think Tim will be able to lower a hook down to us and get him out?"

"He should be able to, the weather is pretty calm right now, but let me radio him and confirm."

Alex radioed Gabe and verified that Tim would be able to come and get Rob and said he would call for Life Flight to meet the ambulance down by Bear Lake so they could get him to Cherryton Hospital quicker. While this was going on Bill had waved Jake over to him. He told Jake about the deputy and how they were going to need to make a run for it if they were going to get out of this now. Before Jake could answer him one of the deputies came over to make sure that Jake was ok and ask him about yesterday. Jake stuck to the story and told the deputy that he had hitchhiked back home and told his dad what had happened. At that point they decided they needed to help.

A few minutes later they could see the helicopter coming around Lakota Peak and headed their direction. Once the helicopter was over the ridge Jared lowered the winch cable and basket down to the EMT's. They moved Rob over to the basket and secured him inside.

"Rob, you need to stay still why they fly you back over to the parking lot. Just close your eyes and relax. The helicopter will have you back to the parking lot in no time and we will get you to the hospital."

The EMT's then made sure Rob was snuggly secured in the gurney basket so he wouldn't fall out.

Rob looked at the EMT and slightly nodded his head in understanding. Alex let Tim know he was good to go and Tim took off back towards the parking lot.

A few minutes later Gabe & the two EMT's that had stayed in the parking lot unhooked Rob from the helicopter cable and onto a waiting gurney. They loaded him up in the ambulance and headed towards their rendezvous point with Life Flight. Gabe then looked up and Steve, Derek and James were coming down the trail.

"Maggie & George, you may want to come out here."

They both came out of the ticket booth and looked at Gabe who pointed at the trailhead. "STEVE" they cried out and went running to him. They both gave him a big hug and looked him over.

"Are you ok my sweet boy?"

"Yes I'm fine other than some cuts. That was so scary." Steve hugged his mom again and started sobbing.

Gabe walked over smiling, he was glad to see the reunion.

"I'm glad we found you Steve, your parents have been worried. Well let me correct that statement. I'm glad you found us. It was very brave of you to make a run for it and go for help."

"Thank you sir."

"You can call me Gabe. Once you have some time with your parents we would like to talk to you so we can get more details about what happened. Is that ok?"

"Can this wait a few days Gabe? I would like him some time to process this before making him relive it again," George asked.

"Yes I suppose that can happen. I will have one of the deputies schedule an appointment with you on Monday. Why don't I have one of these deputies give you a ride back to your camp so you guys can get some rest."

Gabe knew the Sheriff wouldn't be happy with him but he figured it would be best to let the boy get some rest before he was questioned by detectives.

Over on the ridge the group was ready to start hiking back to the parking lot. Alex had spoken with some of the deputies and decided it would be best to have Bill & Jake hike between them so they could keep an eye on them. They weren't buying their story after what they had heard from Steve.

"Alright everyone, it's been a long two days. Let's head back to base camp and get some rest."

"We are going to head back down towards Bridger canyon. Our ATV's are parked down at the trailhead and our truck is parked at the Bridger Mountain ski resort" Bill said.

"Bill, we are going to need to get a statement from you before you leave. Why don't you come with us and we will get you back to your vehicles."

"Can we just come down to the station to give you a statement? We are exhausted."

"No, we really need you to fill out a statement and speak to one of the detectives while you are here."

"Come on Dad, let's just go with them and get this over with."

As they started hiking back Bill was getting even more nervous. He didn't think that the deputies believed his story and he knew that Jake and himself needed to make a run for it if they were going to get away.

"Dad, you're overreacting. Like you said, we just need to keep to our story and we will be fine," Jake whispered.

"What if that Steve kid heard us talking?"

"He didn't, there is no way he could have heard us. If he did, we will say we had searched a different tunnel in the cave before finding Rob and maybe he had heard us while we were down there."

They continued hiking and soon were off the ridge and about to go into the trees when Alex stopped the group.

"Alright, everyone keep your eyes open and stay close to each other, we still haven't found the creature that killed Jim and I don't want anyone else getting hurt."

Bill knew the brush was pretty thick through the middle section of the trail. This would be their best chance to get away if they were going to try.

"Jake, when we get into this thick brush let's just roll down the hillside. I think we can sneak away if we stay at the end of the group and just sneak down the hill."

"Dad, I don't think the opportunity is going to arise, we need to stick to our story. Besides what are we going to do even if we do get away. If we do sneak away they will know we were up to something. Not only that, what are we going to do, live in a cave the rest of our lives? Let's just play it cool and stick to our story, they have no proof that we did anything wrong."

"Ok son you're right, I don't want to live in a cave the rest of our lives. Maybe this will at least buy us some time so we can figure out what to do."

The group continued their hike through the brush and arrived at the parking lot after another thirty minutes.

Gabe was over talking to the Sheriff when he looked up on the hillside and saw Alex and the rest of the group hiking down. They

were the last group to get back to the parking lot. The rest of the
search crews were eating the breakfast that had been brought up by
one of the diners in Bear Lake. They were all ready to head home for
some well deserved rest but needed to be debriefed before leaving.

Gabe and Sheriff walked over to the trailhead and shook Alex's
hand.

"Glad you guys are back, why don't you go and get some
breakfast."

"Glad we are back as well. This is Bill & Jake Appleton, they were
the two that found Rob in the cave."

The Sheriff walked up to them. "I'm Sheriff Hamilton, thank you
for your help finding Rob, we really appreciate it. Why don't you go
grab you some breakfast and one of our detectives will come get you
for a statement. Once we have your statements we will get you to
your vehicles."

Bill nodded his head to the Sheriff and him & Jake headed over
to the breakfast table.

"Gabe, I want you to keep an eye on them, I don't want them
trying to sneak away."

Gabe nodded his head and started following them over to the
breakfast table.

"Bill why don't you put your gun in my truck for safe keeping, I'm
sure your shoulder is tired and you won't need it at the breakfast
table."

"I would prefer to keep it with me."

"I think it would be best to put it in the truck, it will make the
rest of the team feel more at ease."

"I don't give two shits whether they feel at ease or not. My gun
stays with me."

Gabe sighed, "Alright go grab you a plate of food."

Gabe nodded over to the detectives. They had already decided that they were going to interview the two separately and after Bill refusing to give up his rifle they decided right now would be a good time to start.

The two detectives walked over to Bill right as he was picking a plate up.

"Hi I'm Detective Brown & this is Detective Weeks. We would like to get your statement from you so we can continue this investigation."

"Jesus, we haven't had anything to eat yet. Can't you wait a few minutes."

"Why don't you go ahead and fill up your plate and we can then go over to the ticket booth for the interview."

"Alright we will be right over," Jake said trying to defuse the situation.

The two detectives walked away and watched them carefully.

"Dad, you need to keep calm or they aren't going to be on our side."

"I know son, they just piss me off thinking they can tell us where and when to eat, sit, shit. It is ridiculous."

"Just stay calm, play friendly and we can get through this."

They finished filling up their plates and walked over to the detectives.

"Alright Bill, why don't you follow me and we will get your statement first."

"You can't talk to us both at the same time? We were both there together and will have the same story. This is just a waste of time."

"Sorry Bill, just following procedure. Will you please leave your gun with Jake and we can go get your statement? Once you're done we will take you to your vehicles and you will be headed home in no time."

Bill sighed and handed his rifle to Jake and followed the detectives to the ticket booth.

66

It was a long drive from Lakota Cave to Fredericks Basin and Steve had fallen asleep in Maggie's lap on the ride. Maggie had dozed off and on but kept waking to check on Steve. She was relieved he was back safe and was worried about how he was going to handle the trauma he had just been through.

As the truck pulled off the highway onto the dirt road at Fredericks Basin Steve started to wake up. He looked up and saw his mom and smiled and fell back asleep.

Maybe he will handle this better than I thought, Maggie thought.

After driving down the dirt road for what seemed like forever Maggie looked up and saw their camp, everyone was sitting around the campfire waiting for the three to return home. She looked at the clock and it was only 9:30a.m.

George turned around from the front seat and smiled. He was glad that this nightmare was almost over.

The truck pulled into the campground and Clara ran over to the truck.

Maggie slowly shook Steve awake and let him know they were back at camp. He immediately sat up.

"Are we going home or are we staying for the rest of the weekend?"

"We will discuss that in a little bit. I'm sure everyone will be happy to see you.

George reached over to shake the Sheriff's deputy's hand.

"Thank you for the ride back. I will give the Sheriff's office a call to find out when to bring Steve in for a statement on Monday."

The Sheriff's deputy shook George's hand.

"Glad everything worked out for the best."

"I'm sorry about the deputy that was killed, may I ask his name?"

"His name was Jim, he had been with the Sheriff's Dept. for many years."

"Wait, was he working up near Aspen Grove yesterday?"

"Yes he was."

"I spoke with him, while he was searching for those other two boys. That is too bad I really feel for his family."

"I'm just glad he was the only casualty and that we were able to find Steve & Rob alive. That would have made it worth it to Jim."

George, Maggie, & Steve climbed out of the truck and Clara almost knocked them all over trying to get to Steve. She gave him a great big hug and started crying.

"Steve, I was so worried about you!"

Steve hugged her back.

"Glad to see you Clara. You should have seen the beast that took me. It was huge."

By this point everyone had gathered around and they all took turns giving Steve hugs.

"See the paper was right, there was a beast trying to get people."

"You're right Steve, we should have taken it more seriously," George said.

"Did they catch the bad guys, Dad?"

"I believe so son, from what I heard the Sheriff say they are the ones that brought Rob out of the cave."

"Let's go get some breakfast and we can discuss this later."

Charles waved to the deputy as he drove off and Katrina & Gloria went and filled up some plates with breakfast for George, Maggie, & Steve.

They all sat down around the fire and Steve started telling Joey all about the long night he had.

After breakfast there was some discussion on what to do next. They were all exhausted and needed to sleep but also wanted to head home. There had been enough excitement for a decade let alone one weekend.

Everyone went into their trailers and fell quickly asleep. They would decide what to do when they woke up, but for now they needed to sleep.

67

While Bill was in the ticket booth being interviewed by the detectives Gabe was over making small talk with Jake.

"How is Rob, have you heard anything?"

"Well when he left here he wasn't doing very well, but he is in good hands. Let me go see if the Sheriff has heard an update."

While walking over to the Sheriff, Gabe thought of a plan to get Jake to spill the beans on what had happened.

He asked the Sheriff if he had heard any updates on Jake and told him about his plan.

"These two were close friends from what I understand. Let's use this to our advantage. We may be able to pull at Jake's heart string and get him to fess up."

"That's a good idea Gabe. Let's run with it."

Gabe walked back over to Jake.

"Was there an update."

"Yeah, it isn't good they almost lost him in the ambulance but they were able to get his heart started again. He is in good hands, hopefully he will be ok."

Gabe could see the color leave Jake's face.

"Why don't you sit down Jake, I know Rob is a good friend of yours."

Jake sat down and leaned against the tire of Gabe's truck. He leaned the rifle against the truck and Gabe took the opportunity to grab it and put it in his truck.

Jake looked up.

"Just for safekeeping, I will give it back to your Dad when he comes out."

After thirty minutes or so Bill was done being interviewed. He walked out of the ticket booth.

Gabe helped Jake stand up.

"Looks like it's your turn. Just go in there, tell them your side of the story and then you can head home."

Jake nodded his head and started walking towards the ticket booth.

Bill looked over at Jake and winked. He then realized that Jake didn't have the rifle.

"Hey where is my gun?"

"Jake was tired and had sat down so I told him I would put it in the truck for safe keeping.

Let's get Jake's interview over with and you can have your gun back and be on your way.

As Bill & Jake passed each other Bill stopped him and whispered, "Just keep to the story and we will be fine. So far so good."

Jake nodded his head and went into the ticket booth.

"Alright Jake lets get this over with so you can head home and Detective Weeks & I can continue on with our investigation into these attacks. Why don't you tell us about what happened when you and Rob were taken."

Jake nodded his head and started into how. Rob, Becky, & him had gone camping on Wednesday night and how he was attacked and had lost his phone. He explained how on Friday afternoon, himself and Rob had gone to look for his phone and how they were attacked by the beast. He told them how he had gotten away by playing dead and when the beast had left to go attack Rob. He then ran away and made his way to the highway where he had hitchhiked home. Once home his dad and him had decided to go help search for Rob.

As Jake started telling the story about their search Sheriff Hamilton came to the door.

"Detective Brown, can I speak with you & Detective Weeks for a minute?"

"Absolutely Sheriff, pause your story right there Jake and we will be back."

A few minutes later the Detectives walked in with a grim look on their faces.

"Is everything alright Detective?"

"No, unfortunately we just heard that Rob has passed away. I'm so sorry to have to give you that information but since you were his friend I thought you deserved to know."

Jake started sobbing, "This isn't what was supposed to happen, I would have never gone along with this if I knew that Rob and a Deputy would end up dead."

"What do you mean Jake?"

"This isn't how it was supposed to happen."

The detectives looked at each other, they knew the plan was working and they soon would have a confession.

"Alright Jake, what do you mean this wasn't supposed to happen? Have you not been telling us the full truth?"

"We didn't mean for anyone to get hurt."

"Jake, you need to tell us what happened."

"We just meant to scare people out of the valley so our cattle wouldn't be harassed while they grazed."

"We thought if we could get a story in the papers about people being attacked by animals it would keep people out of the canyons."

"Alright Jake so you weren't actually attacked on Wednesday night?"

"No I was. Well it was planned, my dad had brought the beast near the spot we were camping so it could drag me away."

Jake continued on with his story about how they had a shelter built up about one half a mile from the road in Bridger Canyon and how they had been training the beasts to scare people away.

"Alright, Jake I'm confused why don't you start from the beginning."

"It all started a few years ago when we stumbled across the opening to the cave while elk hunting. After hiking to the end of the tunnel we turned around and were on their way back when we came upon the first beast. It ran at us and tried to attack but my dad shot it. After walking up to it we realized he had shot the first bigfoot.

My dad said "We are going to be famous, son. We killed the first bigfoot."

He then had me take his picture with the beast. We then decided to walk down the corridor where the beast had come from and that is where we found the beast lair. Another large beast stood up and charged at us so my dad had raised his gun to shoot it but the beast veered to the right and ran down another corridor. We then walked over to where the beast had been laying and they found three offspring.

I told him "Look dad, there are babies. We are going to be famous for not only killing a bigfoot but also for catching bigfoot!"

My dad picked up one of the baby animals and stared at it for a few minutes.

"You know what son, we need to keep this quiet. If we tell anyone these animals will end up in a zoo and will be of no help to us."

My dad then loaded up the beasts into our backpacks and we headed out of the cave. On the drive home my dad explained his plan. He wanted us to raise the beasts and train them so they could be used to scare off campers and recreationists from this mountain range. His reasoning for this was that he thought the cattle that we were allowed to graze up here for the summer were being harassed and not able to put on as much weight as he would have liked over the summer."

"How did you control the animals and get them to attack?"

"We used a laser pen and would mark where they were supposed to attack. We would mark the location and they would destroy the camp."

"We thought we would test it on Rob and see if we could get it to attack people."

"My dad was up in the trees at Aspen Grove, he had rented a bigfoot suit and used it to grab me. Once he had me out of the way he marked Rob with the laser and one of the beasts grabbed Rob and started attacking him. It then grabbed him and took off towards the cave."

"We didn't know what had happened to Rob so we headed back to camp and then hiked up to the cave and that is where we found Rob at the back of the cave. He seemed ok at that point so we left him and went back to our original plan to try and scare people out of the canyon and we would get him out of the cave later on."

"Ok, how did Steve get taken?"

"We saw his family come into the canyon and they had been riding their UTV's and ATV's all over the place. They were a fairly big group and we thought we could scare them fairly easily so we put our Bigfoot suits on and tried to sneak around and scare the kids. It seemed to work but they were just too inquisitive and nonchalant so we thought we needed to get more forceful. Last night we decided we would have the beasts attack their camp. I snuck down to the camp with one of the beasts on a chain and let it loose. Everything was going according to plan until Steve came out of the trailer. At that point we had no control, the beast took Steve and took off running towards the cave. We tried to catch up but we couldn't so we headed back to the cave as quickly as possible. We never thought anyone would get injured or killed."

"What about the Deputy that was killed? Did you tell the beasts to attack him?"

"No, we didn't have anything to do with that. We don't have the beasts contained, we just know where their lair is, I'm not sure what happened to him."

"Where was your Dad during this?"

"He had stayed back near the cave, we knew that you guys were searching the area and he wanted to be here so if you found the cave he could let me know to go somewhere else.

"Is it possible he released the beast on our deputy?"

"No, I don't think he would do that."

"We have never had a recorded incident with these animals before you guys got involved and you want me to believe that you had nothing to do with it?"

"I understand if you don't believe me, but I have given you the truth, why would I lie about this part of the story?"

Detective Brown stood up and leaned over to Jake, "Your Dad had one of our deputies attacked and he was killed because of your bullshit. You and your Dad are going to be locked up for a long time!"

He then went to the door, opened it up and gave the Sheriff a nod.

The Sheriff knew they had gotten a confession. He walked over to Bill who was sitting on Gabe's tailgate and told him to stand up and turn around.

"Why? What is going on, Bill asked?"

"We know that you were involved in the disappearance of Rob & Steve as well as the death of our deputy. You are under arrest."

"What do you mean?"

Bill started trying to walk away.

"Don't make this harder than it has to be Bill."

Gabe walked up and grabbed Bill's arm and they put him in handcuffs.

They walked him over towards one of the detective's cars and put him in the backseat.

"I want to talk to my son."

"You can talk to him for a minute when he comes out. You realize you ruined his life all for money don't you?"

"I don't know what you are talking about."

"Bill, Jake told us all about your plot to scare people away. He has told us everything so cut the bullshit."

Bill leaned back against the seat with a look of defeat.

A few minutes later Detective Weeks walked Jake out of the ticket booth in handcuffs. He walked him over to the car where Bill was seated.

"I'm sorry Dad, they told me about Rob dying and I couldn't help but break down. He was my friend."

Bill looked at the Sheriff, "Rob's dead?"

"No Rob isn't dead, not yet anyway but we could tell your son had a good heart and may confess if he thought his friend was dead."

"You lied to me!"

"What goes around comes around kid."

Sheriff Hamilton shut the door to the patrol car Bill was in and Gabe walked Jake over to another car. The detectives climbed into their cars and headed towards the jail where Bill & Jake would be held.

Gabe looked over at the Sheriff, "What a weekend."

"Yes and it is only Saturday morning. Let's get this place cleaned up and as soon as the coroner is finished with their investigation we can leave."

68

Steve woke up later that afternoon and looked at the clock, it was 3:30. He looked around and he was the only one in the trailer. He looked out the window and everyone was relaxing and enjoying the sun. Steve walked outside and felt the warmth of the sun. He looked at his family and smiled.

"So are we staying?"

They all laughed and George looked at him. " I think we have all had enough for this camping trip sport. You do have to speak to the detectives on Monday though so we have decided to go into Cherryton and we are all going to stay at the Hampton Inn."

"Wahoo a pool!" Steve said excitedly.

"Is everyone going to stay?"

"Yes everyone is getting a room so we can be together for the next few days, we would hate to break up cousin time.

George and Maggie smiled at each other and they all started packing up to head back to town.

Terry had gone home and got a few hours of sleep and was now headed to the hospital to see how Becky & Rob were doing. He walked into the hospital and asked about Rob's status. The nurse said that he was in an induced coma but they expected him to be okay. He then asked if Becky was still in her room and if he could go visit.

The nurse rang Becky's room in the ICU and spoke to Becky's dad and then she hung up the phone.

"Trevor said Becky is currently awake and would be happy to see you."

Terry thanked the nurse and walked back to the ICU where Trevor met him.

"How are you Trevor?"

"I'm doing well, we just got the news that they will be moving Becky out of the ICU later tonight."

"That is great news, have you heard about Rob?"

"I heard on the news that he had been found and was brought to the hospital, but I haven't seen him yet."

"Have you told Becky?"

"No, I was waiting to hear his status before giving her any hope."

" I just spoke to the nurse up front and she said Rob was in an induced coma but expected to make a full recovery."

"Well, that is much better that I had expected. Why don't we go in and tell her & Diana the news."

They both walked into Becky's hospital room.

Diana & Becky both looked at Terry and said hello.

"Becky, you are looking much better than when I saw you yesterday, how are you feeling?"

"I'm feeling a little better, have you found Rob?"

Terry looked at Trevor and he gave him a nod to continue on.

"Yes we have found Rob and he here at the hospital."

"Is he ok?"

"He is currently in a coma but from what the Doctors say he will be fine."

"I want to see him."

"Honey, once they get him stabilized and you're moved to your new room maybe you can go visit him." Trevor interjected.

"Ok" Becky said, still too tired to put up much of a fight.

"What happened to them?" Becky asked.

"Well that is a long story that we are still trying to sort out."

"Once we have all of the details we can give you more information. I'm glad you are healing Becky, I will stop by in the next day or two to get more information from you."

"Thanks Officer Johnson."

Terry smiled and walked out of the room. He walked down the hallway and looked into Rob's room and he looked peaceful, but Terry knew he was fighting for his life. Terry walked over to the nurses station and asked about Rob. The nurse told him the neurologist was on his way down to do a full assessment.

"Are his parents here?" Terry asked.

"No but they are on their way and should be here shortly."

Terry thanked the nurse for the information and headed outside. Terry walked through the doors and felt the summer sun on his face. He decided it was time to head home and have a well-deserved drink with Joselyn.

Meanwhile back up at Lakota cave the Detectives and coroner had finished up their investigation. As the coroner brought Jim's body out from the trail everyone that was still there lined up and saluted their former co-worker and friend. They loaded his body into the coroner's vehicle and it headed down the canyon with two deputies escorting the coroner's van to Cherryton.

Just as the Sheriff was climbing into his truck Gabe walked over to him.

"What are we going to do about these animals that are running around?" Gabe asked.

"Well Gabe, that is your jurisdiction, but my opinion is other than random pictures every so often we have never had any violent run-ins with them before. I say let them be.

He reached his hand out the window and shook Gabe's hand and thanked him for his dedication. He then started up his truck and drove off.

Gabe looked out at the mountain range, trees beginning to leaf out and wild flowers beginning to blossom. He smiled and thought to himself.

"Well I guess we have solved one big mystery. Bigfoot really does exist."

1/30/2024

Printed in Great Britain
by Amazon